Margaret froze at the short, sharp ringing sound, as though someone had struck stone with metal. This did come from the back of the garden, and all Margaret wished to do was to depart immediately.

As she reached the archway, she looked back. It was with utter surprise that she saw the huge left-hand urn topple over and crash to the ground. She could feel the vibration under her feet as tons of marble met the earth.

Margaret closed her eyes quickly and opened them. There was something under the toppled urn. Someone...

Also by Joyce Christmas
Published by Fawcett Gold Medal Books:

DARK TIDE

SUDDENLY IN HER SORBET

SIMPLY TO DIE FOR

Joyce Christmas

FAWCETT GOLD MEDAL • NEW YORK

For two truly distinguished families:

The Smiths: Dad and Marie
The Nelsons: Marci, Chris, Pat, and Greg

A Fawcett Gold Medal Book
Published by Ballantine Books
Copyright © 1989 by Joyce Christmas

Library of Congress Catalog Card Number: 89-91308

ISBN 0-449-14539-5

Manufactured in the United States of America

First Edition: November 1989

Chapter 1

*W*hen the phone rings in midsummer in Manhattan, she who answers is courting social death. Simply no one who's anyone admits to being in the city in late July.

On the other hand, when Lady Margaret Priam answered the phone in her spacious East Side apartment on the hottest day of the year, she did so with total indifference to New York social rules. Titled English ladies of very good family, good looks, and only a few years beyond thirty do not fear death by social gaffe. They have been bred to rise above anything life in New York might offer. But not even Lady Margaret imagined that merely by answering a telephone she might overstep the boundaries of acceptable behavior—just a bit—by becoming involved with a murderer.

"Hello?" Margaret was wary. Since it was early in the day, she supposed it would be a person selling banking services, time-shares in Florida, or something equally useless to her.

"Margaret, thank God you haven't gone off somewhere like everyone else. I need you desperately."

It took a moment for Margaret to understand that it was Lynne Jordan speaking. A glossy denizen of New York society, an acquaintance more than a friend. Contemporary in years, but she suspected that Lynne's claim to thirty-two was a bit too low.

"I didn't dare go out to the Hamptons until *It* has been settled," Lynne said breathlessly. She did not elaborate on the nature of *It*. "I've missed George's fireworks, and I

1

can't tell you how many really important parties. I think Mort Zuckerman is entertaining—"

"Is he?" Margaret said. "I never thought so." She did not much care for Lynne, although they had been thrown together often enough in the past couple of years at the public and private affairs rich New Yorkers seem to enjoy and to which unattached, aristocratic English expatriates are eagerly invited.

"Listen, darling," Lynne said, "it's a matter of life and death. At least it looks like the death of me unless you can help."

"What might I be able to do, Lynne?" Margaret asked cautiously. What she did know about Lynne was that she was an accomplished manipulator, able to coerce the most recalcitrant haute couture designer into giving her a hefty discount on a top-of-the-line evening dress (although an outright gift was preferable). She was capable of black-mailing a *dear* friend into buying tickets for an entire table at a charity affair; willing to bribe a maître d' into giving her the best location in the restaurant; shameless about claiming intimacy with the brightest stars of the more well-publicized circles of New York society.

Margaret was unsure about exactly what gave Lynne her social leverage, but it was not an excess of breeding. Although Lynne seemed to be presently unmarried, there had certainly been a rich husband once, providing a divorce settlement to support her stylish life-style now.

"We must lunch," Lynne said.

"Well . . . yes," Margaret said. "Lunch sometime would be nice. I am rather minding Kasparian's affairs while he's abroad buying, but I'm not terribly busy." A small fib. Bedros Kasparian's Madison Avenue antique shop where Margaret assisted was closed for the summer. Kasparian had no affairs to speak of. "When?"

"Why, today. As soon as possible. I told you it was life or death, and it's difficult to postpone either. That new Italian restaurant people are talking about, Enrico's. In the East Sixties. It's different from the usual."

It would, Margaret knew, truly be death to show up at

an Institution like Le Cirque or Mortimer's in the summertime. Someone might see that Lynne wasn't holidaying in another hemisphere.

"All right. One o'clock?" Margaret could manage an hour and a half at an overpriced-though-likely-not-too-nourishing lunch, in surroundings excruciatingly tasteful. The menu would be large in dimensions, although limited in the written word.

"Wonderful," Lynne said and sounded almost grateful. "If you get there first, make sure Enrico gives you one of the good banquettes. Near the front."

Margaret did not like to think that she was the sole human being in New York City to whom Lynne Jordan could turn in a time of trouble, but perhaps she was.

As proof of the emptiness of Manhattan, there was on her desk a stack of invitations and phone messages from holidaying friends urging her to visit in the Hamptons, Nantucket, Aspen, the Napa Valley, Provence ("We have a place so fabulously off the tourist trail you'll never see a soul, I promise!"), a yacht cruising the Greek islands.

There was even a desperate note from her young and quite platonic friend, Paul Castrocani, son of an impoverished Italian prince and a Texas millionairess now safely remarried to one of her own kind. Paul was dutifully visiting his mother and stepfather in Dallas to charm them into raising his allowance. "It is truly awful here. Please feel welcome to visit," he had written. He had heavily underlined the word *please*.

But she had rejected sun, sea, mountains, and Texas luxury. She preferred to lounge aimlessly in the city, not quite admitting she hoped for the return of a man who had engaged her interest in recent months. He was visiting parents retired to a bucolic corner of New Jersey but had not invited her along, claiming they were not prepared to meet a genuine English lady, sister to an earl and even mentioned in society columns.

When Margaret reached the restaurant before Lynne, Enrico did not require persuasion to seat her at a conspicuous table, for the place was not filled. Indeed, those who

were there were certainly not Ladies Who Lunch but
strollers enticed inside on that hot day by the cool white
interior—and probably not by the double-digit prices on
everything from tiny plates of greens to minuscule bowls of
pasta.

Enrico himself had the look of a man merely hanging on
until it was time to close up for August and take wing with
his ill-gotten gains to an Italian lakeside.

Lynne Jordan entered as though expecting applause.
She was dressed in pale pink linen, tastefully bejeweled,
and thin. Thin as sin. Her cheek came to within a practiced
nano-space of Margaret's, but no skin made contact, so
artful makeup was not disturbed, nor one dark hair on
Lynne's coiffed head.

"Lovely to see you," Lynne said, but Margaret could
not be sure that she was not commenting on the handsome,
very young waiter. "San Pellegrino, lime. *Insalata* with
radicchio, vinaigrette, and make sure the chef gives me
aceto balsamico. Three small shrimp."

The waiter was impassive in the face of such gastro-
nomic assurance. "And for you, *signorina?*"

"Tortellini primavera, plenty of tortellini," Margaret
said. "White wine. And three small shrimp."

"How do you manage to stay so ... trim? I put on
pounds and pounds if I even *think* of pasta." There was in
Lynne's tone the implication that Margaret could trim
down to a size four if she would dedicate herself to reaching the brink of starvation. "I've scarcely laid eyes on you
in months. That party for the maharajah in February,
wasn't it? You came alone. Are you seeing anyone?"

"Yes, in a manner of speaking," Margaret said.

"That's good," Lynne said. She seemed relieved that
Margaret was suitably involved, but she was not about to
allow Margaret's personal life to interfere with her own
pressing needs. "Listen," she said. "I have a terrible problem, and I know I can depend on you. It's Camilla Stafford. And Daniel Stafford and Eloise."

Margaret nodded. It was some variation on the inevita-
ble Eternal Triangle whose dimensions were not yet clear.

"And me, naturally," Lynne added.

All right, an Eternal Rectangle. And if life and death, who was planning to shoot whom? Margaret resolutely signaled the waiter for another glass of white wine to help her through the list of names. "Please begin again, Lynne. I'm afraid I'm confused."

"You must know Daniel Stafford."

The name rang familiar. Margaret conjured up a face from a dinner party in the spring. There had been cocktails three dozen stories above the mean streets, groups of men in black tie and women showing off the best their closets had to offer, and yes, Daniel Stafford.

"Graying—no, white—hair," Margaret said, "but youthful. Does something with money, has it or makes it for others. Very attractive." She recalled that he had been very attractive indeed, and possibly had made a pass at her, right before their hostess had signaled the way into dinner. There had been some light conversation, establishing his financial position (sound) and social credentitals (lofty). They had not crossed paths since that evening.

"That's Dan. A *wonderful* man." Her expression was positively lustful. "His wife was my sister Ann, Camilla's mother. Ann died four years ago, when Camilla was about fourteen."

"How sad. That was before I came to New York to live." Some little memory of a scandal linked to the Stafford name nudged into her consciousness and vanished.

"For the past four years, I've rather stood in as Camilla's mother figure."

Not my idea of Mother, Margaret thought.

"It was the least I could do for my only niece," Lynne said. "A terrible tragedy. Now I don't know what to do."

Margaret said, slowly and clearly, "What is the problem? And who, may I ask, is Eloise?" The tortellini was excellent, topped with miniature carrots, tiny peas, petite haricots, an array of baby vegetables that had never been allowed to grow up. A pity to waste the pleasure of it with a tangled family tragedy.

Lynne beckoned the waiter with a commanding forefinger topped by a pearly, perfect nail and recklessly ordered another glass of expensive foreign water.

"Eloise Stafford is Daniel's mother, Camilla's grandmother on the Stafford side. The problem is that she insists that Camilla make her debut at the balls this winter."

"Well, yes. That would be important to a grandmother."

"And I couldn't agree with her more." Margaret had the impression that Lynne seldom agreed with her late sister's mother-in-law. "It's so difficult these days for children to know the *right* sort of people. And Camilla is a bit . . . backward for her age. Stubborn. She doesn't want to be a debutante. As if a child of that age knows anything at all. She has some odd notion that she ought to be doing good for others." Lynne wrinkled her possibly reshaped little nose in disgust.

Margaret had been a so-called debutante during one London Season more than a decade and a half before. She had rather enjoyed it, but the fact that a young woman of good family preferred not to become a debutante seemed like no terrible crisis.

"The terrible crisis," Lynne said, "is that I simply don't have the time to talk Camilla into coming out and then to see her through it all. That's *six months* out of my life. And all those dreadful, boring details."

Heaven forbid that this self-proclaimed mother figure should have her life upset doing what mother figures are supposed to do. Margaret was beginning to see a clearer picture.

"You want me to convince Camilla that making her debut with all its attendant possibilities for a rosy future is worth it," Margaret said. "And then you want me to see her through it. Sort of a surrogate mother figure."

"Exactly. How clever! Ann would have wanted it for her. Daniel has a sister . . ." Lynne paused. "Well, you know about her. Not at all suitable." Margaret didn't know, but let it pass. "Daniel's brother Toby is no help."

"I understand there are professionals who do that sort of thing. Debutante balls and the like." Margaret was certain there was more to come, soon to be revealed. There was.

Lynne said, "Heavens, we would *never* want one of those women. We want *you*. Eloise herself came up with your name."

Margaret thought about that. "I don't believe I've met Mrs. Stafford."

"Eloise doesn't go about in society as she once did, but she keeps track of all the really good people," Lynne said. "Please say yes. We'll see that you are very well repaid for your trouble."

Margaret liked that. Nothing so crass as being "paid" to do a job, but "repaid" for doing a kindness. Since she lived on a modest family inheritance and a modest salary from Kasparian and had found that living in some comfort in New York required a good deal of money, she didn't find the idea of compensation offensive. What she didn't like was the idea that if she helped thrust Camilla Stafford into the adult world, remove her as Daddy's responsibility, Daddy would have time for his dead wife's sister.

"How did your sister happen to die?" Margaret asked. "She must have been quite young."

Lynne toyed with a fragment of radicchio left on her plate.

"Actually," she said, "she was murdered."

A longish pause ensued. Margaret wanted to press for the details—for example, murdered by whom, and how—but Lynne did not seem eager to elaborate.

"Please do say you will help us all out," Lynne said. "Your social position is . . . impeccable."

"I'd have to look at my calendar," Margaret told Lynne. "The holidays are so frightfully busy." She waved a hand vaguely to signify the overwhelming crush of social obligations six months ahead, when the debutante balls would be in full swing.

"I do understand," Lynne said. "Look, isn't that Dana Canby? She told everybody she was spending the whole summer on Fisher's Island. I can't believe it! She's had a few tucks taken. Those eyelids look too unreal."

"About Camilla," Margaret said.

"I know you'll find a way, darling. You're too good,

and with all that little trouble in the family when Ann died and afterwards, Camilla needs real clout to get her to the right parties *and* the Junior Cotillion. That's the important ball."

"I'll call you," Margaret said. That an accident of birth had given her "clout" in New York social circles would have dismayed Margaret's late mother, the Countess of Brayfield. Margaret herself found it amusing. "About your sister's murder," Margaret began, but the expression on Lynne's face stopped her. It was not exactly a smile, nor was it a smirk. It was the look of a woman who was secretly glad that she was the survivor in a hard-fought competition.

"It's over and done with, and there's no point in discussing it. A case of random violence. I don't know what this world is coming to with people like that out there. The family has tried to forget." Lynne now had readjusted her face to look appropriately sad.

"Except Camilla? Perhaps the idea of a debut reminds her of what her mother wanted for her."

"I don't think so," Lynne said. "Camilla isn't a thinker. She doesn't care about good clothes and knowing the right people. Her father and I have tried to channel her interests in the right direction. Her grandmother Eloise is a wonderful role model, but she and Camilla don't really get along. That's why we need you."

Margaret saw that Lynne was still trying to detect whether the lady lunching across the room had been tucked and tightened.

"I wish you'd meet poor Camilla at least. It would be a kindness," Lynne said. "I've had trouble reaching the . . . the *real* Camilla lately."

"I could do that," Margaret said warily, "meet her, that is to say." She wondered if she was allowing herself to be manipulated by an expert without a struggle. "But I make no promises."

"You *are* an angel." Lynne was satisfied. She summoned the waiter for the check. "I'll have my secretary call you tomorrow. We'll settle everything so I can get out of the city. This heat is outrageous. Lovely to see you. I must dash."

Lynne was away and across the room for a closer inspection of her friend, not quite touching cheeks, exclaiming, tossing her head back gaily.

Margaret slipped away. Enrico stood at the doorway, hands behind his back, and contemplated the empty, heat-scorched sidewalk in front of his establishment.

Chapter 2

"*Don't get* into trouble while I am away." The last words Bedros Kasparian had spoken to Margaret before he caught his flight abroad. Then he had smiled benevolently at her, a foot shorter than she and perhaps forty years older. "That nice De Vere fellow you're seeing ought to keep you in line."

"He's gone to New Jersey," Margaret had said. "Actually I don't see that much of him. He also warned me to stay out of trouble."

"You see? We understand you."

After lunching with Lynne Jordan, Margaret wondered if Kasparian and De Vere would define "trouble" as consenting to launch into society a reluctant debutante with a murdered mother in her history.

Margaret herself had certain reluctant feelings. De Vere would never agree to accompany her to any such social event as a debutante ball, since he was extremely firm about not escorting her to what he called Affairs, Fetes, Galas, and Other Self-Indulgent Displays of Undeserved Affluence. And he was a busy man, since he happened to be a police detective whom she had met the previous fall when she stepped into the deep waters surrounding the murder of a highly visible doyenne of New York society.

Then she decided that murder of any sort must be a fairly rare occurrence in high social circles, even in America. Her curiosity was stirred.

A dozen blocks north, a block or so west lay answers to questions that had not been answered, nor even asked, during lunch. Margaret thought that Poppy Dill, who wrote a society column for one of the city newspapers and who knew everything about everybody in that world, could be persuaded to share old gossip about these Staffords. Poppy seldom left the comforts of her apartment, except to make an annual pilgrimage upstate to Saratoga during the August racing season, and now and then to go abroad to invade the ancestral homes of titled and famous friends. Margaret could almost count on her being at home today.

"How nice to have a caller!" Poppy was delighted to see her. She was a small, silver-haired woman dressed in the kind of frilly peignoir one imagined Barbara Cartland imagined was suitable at-home wear for her romantic heroines. "I loathe summertime. Everyone leaves town and there's no one to drop by."

She led Margaret into her cool boudoir where she wrote out her "Social Scene" columns and held court for daily visitors during the seasons when the social focus was on New York.

"I'm surprised you're not away," Poppy said and waited to be told why. Every fragment of information was important to her.

"I'm looking after Kasparian's business while he's abroad."

"The shop is closed. It's that young man, isn't it?"

"Partly." Margaret left it at that. She wasn't sure how serious she was about De Vere, and she wasn't going to give Poppy an item for tomorrow's column. "I had a note from Paul Castrocani."

"The prince is a dear boy," Poppy said. "I *must* see if I can find him a suitable young woman. It's a shame you're a bit too old for him. He must be what? Twenty-five?"

"He manages well enough on his own," Margaret said. She did not add that, to Paul, "suitable" meant obscenely wealthy. "Poppy, do you know anything about the death of Ann Stafford four years ago?"

"Of course," Poppy said complacently. "Would you like some iced tea? Or a nice Tom Collins?"

"Nothing, thank you. I had lunch today with Ann's sister, Lynne Jordan, and she mentioned the murder."

Poppy had a faraway look. "Murder. One always thinks of murder as being a premeditated sort of thing. It should be called something different when someone is stabbed in her own home by a robber or a drug addict or a lunatic. . . ."

"Is that what happened?"

"So they say. No one was ever caught or accused or tried and convicted." Poppy looked at her shrewdly. "I never believed we heard the whole story. At first there was some idea that it was someone Ann knew. Even before it happened, certain people were spreading rumors about boyfriends. I looked into that *very* carefully. Possible, but nothing that I could find out." Poppy's expression suggested that if she had found nothing, there was nothing to be found. "Daniel is a different story. He had his not-so-secret affairs with some rather well-known women before Ann died. For whatever reason, she put up with it, although I would have divorced him on the spot. Nowadays he squires a lot of women about, the usual thing."

"About the murder . . ."

"A fabulous sensation for a time." Poppy became almost breathless in recounting it. "Ann was alone at the Stafford summer estate in Cranford, Connecticut. The family has spent every summer there for years and years. Someone broke in to rob the place and ended up killing her. Actually, she wasn't quite alone. Little Camilla was about, off playing with a friend. Came home and found her mother dead. Room overturned, a few bits and pieces stolen. Nasty. The family rushed to her side and tried to keep it quiet. Without success, I might add, so they pretend even yet that it didn't happen. Eloise Stafford—Daniel's mother—was simply furious about the murder. Her sort doesn't care for headlines. The sort she became, that is. She likes to forget that she married above herself, thanks to a nouveau riche and ambitious family. The press had a field day with her debut in the midst of the Depression. Incredibly expensive and in perfectly terrible taste. I was just a young reporter, but I remember it well."

Poppy leaned back on the pile of cushions on the chaise where she reclined and looked at Margaret thoughtfully.

"I wonder," Poppy said, "why you are asking me this."

Margaret decided to tell her. Poppy's good will would be important if Margaret decided to help thrust Camilla into society. Among hundreds of debutantes, only a few could be mentioned in the society pages.

"Another debut. Lynne asked me to take charge of Camilla for the next few months, leading up to her debut at the Junior Cotillion. Apparently Mrs. Stafford herself decided I was the one, and sent Lynne on an errand to plead my cooperation."

"Lynne Jordan remains a nobody, no matter how hard she tries. Conspicuous consumer of luxury goods. Heart like a lump of coal," Poppy said. "The type who's always currying favor with the Eloise Staffords of this world. I can't abide her."

Margaret herself did not feel especially warm about Lynne, but certainly she made good copy for Poppy. "Social Scene" regularly took note that she gave parties, attended parties, found her way onto charity committees, was seen at openings, flew off on the Concorde to view the Paris designers' fall and spring collections or to Gstaad for skiing.

"She is not a lady," Poppy said. "You find a lot of that in New York nowadays. Lynne and Ann—their name was Harris—were nobody to speak of. From California or Arizona, I'd have to look it up. They came to New York and were taken up by the right people. Now, Ann was gorgeous. She completely enraptured Daniel Stafford and ended up marrying him. You'd think Eloise would have been more sympathetic to Ann, given their similar backgrounds. Lynne ended up marrying Philip Jordan. You *must* know him. Tons of money, and all those Rembrandts and Van Goghs. Of course Philip is known for marrying anything that moves upright on two legs. Didn't last long, but he can afford any number of marital mistakes."

"Lynne says she's been like a mother to Camilla since Ann died."

Poppy hooted with laughter. "She is definitely *not* the motherly type. But she has always had an eye on the father. She's been after Daniel since she laid eyes on him. She still is, especially now that he's free. Trust me. I have a sense for that kind of thing." Poppy beamed happily.

"Poor Camilla." Margaret was not at all interested in Lynne's lusts.

Poppy shook her head. "Eloise must be thinking that a nice, conventional debut will make up for the fact that Daniel betrayed the family by marrying an unsuitable woman who had the poor taste to be murdered. I'm not one to repeat gossip," Poppy said without irony, "but people actually wondered at the time if the child might have been party to the murder. You know what these women are like when they get to talking at lunch." Poppy leaned forward confidentially. "I don't see Camilla in a divine little white gown tripping gaily down the grand staircase. She's actually been known to run away to . . . God knows where." Poppy sniffed her distaste for the idea of leaving the comforts of home for places unknown. "These young people involved in the debutante scene are frightful snobs. I'm afraid she would have a very unhappy time of it. I doubt that she was brought up to have the correct debutante mentality. A successful deb must love her work *and* be totally acceptable to the old dragons who decide who is to be invited to which ball. They can be very difficult women, although they are all very dear friends of mine."

"According to Lynne, Camilla isn't at all interested."

"The whole point is to have a good time with your friends and meet suitable young men of good family. If she's not interested, it seems a frightful waste of time and money."

"Should I do it?" Margaret asked and was sincerely interested in Poppy's judgment.

Poppy looked at her sternly. "The Staffords are *said* to have piles of money. They live very well. Most of it is tied up in trusts, as I recall. Camilla's grandfather, old Gus Stafford, was only half a fool. I assume they offered to pay you."

"Something of the sort was mentioned."

"That's good. It will be a lot of uphill work."

"But it's only a New York debut. . . ."

"Yes, but remember you'll have to deal with the whole family. My impression has always been that they are perpetually spoiled children who insist on having it their way. If you like a challenge, then go ahead. There are likely to be problems. These debuts are planned years and years in advance. You have to have lists and lists of young people from the really nice families. Camilla would have to be on other people's lists to be invited to the good parties and then be invited to come out at one of the big balls."

"I've agreed to meet Camilla."

"Do that, and then decide. I'm curious to know what she's really like. You never hear of her being involved in the little activities New York children of that class seem to enjoy."

Poppy walked over to her desk where her old typewriter rested. She straightened some pens and shuffled some papers. Then she said, "That family and its affairs have always interested me. Not simply the fact of the murder. Like a lot of those families, they struggle to seem so perfect on the surface, but one knows that something ghastly is always going on underneath. That's especially true of the Staffords."

Poppy opened a drawer in her desk and took out a folder. "I had out my file on the family only this week. It seems to me about time that Daniel remarried. They need to have some Stafford sons to carry on the name. Lynne would like to be the bride, but I doubt that will happen. Daniel escorts her about a bit, but I can't help but feel that's because Lynne has arranged it so. I do know that Eloise would like to see him marry again." She gazed at Margaret. "To someone terribly suitable."

Margaret laughed. "Me? I met him but once, and I

hardly think I'm an ideal candidate for marriage."

"You're young, you're attractive, you have a very distinguished lineage. Eloise must think you are perfect."

"You do know everything," Margaret said admiringly.

Poppy made a dismissive gesture. "I try," she said. "Lord knows I try." Poppy decided to arrange herself decoratively on her chaise against a pile of satin pillows. She opened her file folder. "Now, you will be interested in the house in Cranford where the murder took place. A little way beyond Greenwich, on Long Island Sound. It's been in the Stafford family since year one. A summer palace with thirty rooms and a grand view of the Sound. The Cranford area used to be quite an exclusive summer colony, some very fine families, but everyone important has sold off their property to stockbrokers and doctors and the like. You'll have to see the place."

"Why so?"

Poppy's look of feigned surprise amused Margaret. "I thought you had a taste for tracking down murderers," she said. "At least that has been my experience."

"No," Margaret said firmly. "No murders."

"Aren't you the tiniest bit curious? Wealthy young matron brutally slain. . . ." Poppy was sounding like a tabloid headline. "Seriously, you'll have to look it over for the party."

"What party would that be?"

Poppy was astonished. "There would be *no* way to introduce the girl to the right young people without entertaining a pack of them informally, but at great expense, before the coming-out season, preferably in a remote spot where the damage will not be so obvious."

"You are undoubtedly correct," Margaret said.

"Yes, I am," Poppy said complacently. "Now, take these clippings I've collected about the family. I wouldn't trust anyone but you to return them safely."

"I don't think I need to. . . ." But Margaret reached out and took the folder. "I'll just keep them a day or two," she said.

* * *

When Margaret reached home late in the afternoon, the doorman presented her with a package delivered by the U.S. Mail truck.

She considered herself worldly and sophisticated, a grown women with a divorce half a dozen years in her past, a person admired by virtue of the name she bore by those who did not know her and genuinely liked by those who did. Mature, reasonably stable. Yet her heart jumped when she saw the package was from De Vere.

Margaret turned up the air conditioning in her apartment and saw that a message had been left on her answering machine. Lynne Jordan had allowed no grass to grow under her Maud Frizon shoes: "Camilla is coming in from Connecticut the day after tomorrow. You will be lunching with her and Mrs. Stafford at the Staffords' residence at one." Lynne had left the Stafford address on East Sixty-third Street. It seemed that she assumed Margaret's participation was *un fait accompli*. The manipulator had triumphed. Margaret did not care much for a first meeting with Camilla in the company of her formidable grandmother.

She unwrapped the package and found a note from De Vere:

> *This object is a representation in crude tin of the Taj Mahal, Monument to Love Eternal. I don't know how it found its way to a flea market in New Jersey. However, if you turn the dome, you will see that it is talented.*

Margaret turned the dome of the Taj Mahal and a music box inside played "Raindrops Keep Fallin' on My Head."

Margaret smiled. De Vere was not good at expressing emotions in words, but he had a way of utilizing the random inanimate object to indicate his feelings. She was rather glad to assume by this token that he missed her, as she missed him.

She turned eagerly to Poppy's file on the Staffords, and discovered anew that there were things that went on behind many walls in New York City that no lady should care to know about.

Ann's murder had been headline material. Big, black headlines, with the words *brutal, posh, wealthy, slain, exclusive,* and *in cold blood* prominent in various combinations. It had been reported as Poppy described: pretty, young, socially prominent wife of handsome, wealthy, socially prominent businessman ("manages family interests") surprises unknown, deranged criminal intent on stripping the lavish Stafford estate of its priceless knickknacks and is stabbed, bludgeoned, strangled. . . .

There was a passing mention of the victim's young daughter, and much shock and disbelief that the cruel realities of life could impinge so violently on innocent and privileged lives.

Innocent victim—perhaps. Margaret examined a grainy photo of the alleged murder scene—a shot of a long, sunny room with comfortable chairs, gleaming floor, and thickets of tall potted plants—and thought Ann might not have been terribly bright. Margaret would have taken the first opportunity to scamper to safety if she had come upon a bloodthirsty intruder.

Gradually the story died away into smaller and smaller paragraphs. By the time it disappeared from the press, there had been no resolution, forgotten by all but the likes of Poppy and society gossips with long memories.

Daniel's brother Toby was mentioned frequently in social columns collected from the late seventies and early eighties. A habitué of the discos of the day, a member of junior committees, the escort of publicity-hungry "actresses." News stories reporting two incidents of exuberant youthful high spirits, but all was forgiven. A car accident, with Toby unharmed and companions less fortunate. Exonerated. He seemed a case of overprivileged irresponsibility. Then he disappeared from print for a time and reemerged reborn as a jazz musician. There was a fairly recent mimeographed flyer addressed to Poppy about his jazz group in performance at a downtown club. Toby seemed to be a pianist.

She found a bundle of clippings announcing sister Nancy's marriages, divorces, and other liaisons. Very colorful, conveying the distinct impression of a spoiled, rich, and now-aging brat. The press had given up on her frequently changing names: she was always simply Nancy Stafford.

The old *Times* announcement of the marriage of Daniel Stafford of New York City and Cranford, Connecticut, to Ann Harris of Fresno was brief. The groom's Stafford and other important connections were noted. The bride did not seem to have any family connections at all. The wedding had not been a major social event.

Then Margaret found, at the bottom of the pile, some fragile, yellowing clippings dating from Eloise Stafford's youth. Camilla's grandmother had been a beauty from a family that seemed to have bought its way into the society of the day.

How little things change, Margaret thought, as she read about Eloise's lavish debut in the midst of the Depression, and then her glittering marriage to the eventually very distinguished Augustus Stafford (now a dozen years deceased according to his lengthy *Times* obituary), their departure via ocean liner for a European honeymoon, grand parties at the Connecticut summer house. One story was devoted to the house itself: the titled guests (ranging from the indefatigable Windsors to deposed Balkan monarchs), the number of rooms, the architectural details, the imported statuary, the rose garden, the topiary garden, the tennis courts and the children's playhouse, the stables, the acres of land surrounding the house, the number of servants required to maintain the establishment.

Margaret stopped reading and thought for a moment.

The ring of her telephone shook her from the contemplation of the Staffords.

"I'm glad to find you home," De Vere said. "I've been summoned back to the city. A big and messy case has been handed to me."

"How soon, then?" Margaret asked. She was pleased that he was returning.

"Tomorrow, but I won't be free at all for some days."

"Ah." Pleasure became disappointment. He had once

told her that being married to a policeman had made his former wife a bit crazy. Even with their uneven and not yet very intimate relationship, she could understand that.

"We'll meet when we can," she said gamely. Her eye fell on a screaming tabloid headline about Ann's murder. "Do you have any recollection of a murder at a Connecticut estate four or so years ago? A woman by the name of Ann Stafford, from a very prominent family? Never solved as far as I can judge."

"Lady Margaret Priam does not need to know about a murder," De Vere said sternly. "Not anything. No matter who did what to whom."

"But do you remember it? Stafford."

He relented a bit. "Not professionally. I only know what I read in the papers at the time. One of those cases where a crazed young criminal breaks in for what he can loot and comes up against an innocent bystander. Usually it's the maid dusting the antiques."

"Hmm. Curious. I was just struck by that. I wonder where the servants were."

"What?" De Vere sounded puzzled.

"Nothing. I'm only curious because someone asked me to help a girl socially. Her mother was the victim."

"Don't speak of victims to me, Margaret. You promised never to involve yourself in serious matters."

Margaret narrowed her eyes. "I'd forgotten," she said. "Serious matters are not my strong suit."

"You know what I mean," he said. "I don't want anything to happen to you."

Later she decided it was then that she was overcome by a need to see that house in Connecticut. She had to see the place where Ann Stafford was murdered.

"Why don't you call me as soon as you have some time," she told De Vere cheerfully. "I've missed you."

Chapter 3

After the rush hour into Manhattan, the roadways out of the city to Connecticut are crowded but not impossible. Once on the Connecticut Turnpike, the masters of the road are the eighteen-wheelers tearing into the heart of New England.

Margaret, still a well-conditioned English drive-on-the-left driver, liked the turnpike, because with multiple lanes it didn't matter much where one drove.

The day after her lunch with Lynne and the day before another with Camilla, she was on her way to Cranford, Connecticut, to catch a glimpse of the Stafford house on the Sound where Ann had died and perhaps even a glimpse of Camilla. She thought if the situation became sticky, she could blither her way out of it—talk about seeing the layout of the house for the party, whatever. In any case, the beaches of Connecticut sounded enticing.

The car she seldom used but paid a fortune to park in the garage of her building gave an extra excuse: exercise the auto the way she used to exercise the horses back home in England at Priam's Priory.

The Cranford exit was upon Margaret sooner than she expected. The exit ramp curved around and brought her to a country road lined with maples and oaks with thick trunks that indicated they had stood for a century or more. Spacious, white turn-of-the-century houses stood back from the road on broad lawns. A short drive brought Margaret into the center of town: a New England classic with village green and white Congregational church, a quaint railroad station that served commuters to and from Manhattan, shops displaying subdued suburban matrons' clothes in lime green and strawberry. The cars correctly parked at an angle to Main Street were Mercedes and BMWs, Audis and the occasional station wagon. A prosperous, orderly town, with the summer people (all those stockbrokers and doctors) kept in their place.

Margaret pulled into an empty space near the railroad station. Outside the car it was hot but refreshing. The heat came from the sun overhead in the clear blue sky, not from concrete walls and sidewalks exhaling unhealthy urban breath. She caught the faint tang of the sea.

The immediate problem was locating the Stafford estate. She examined passersby. The young woman with two small children was harried. An older woman eyed Margaret's white silk shirt and skirt and gold sandals suspiciously. A teenage boy in cutoffs and a Grateful Dead T-shirt looked reasonably alert.

"Stafford?" He blinked at her upper-class English accent. "It's, like, a mile out of town, near the Sound. You take Main Street to the intersection and turn right at the gas station. There's this road, Stafford Road, on the left. You follow it to the end. The house is past the stone gates."

Margaret said, "I understand it's a large house."

"Mr. Kessler sells houses," the boy said, misunderstanding. He pointed across the street to a mock colonial building with a sign reading CRANFORD REAL ESTATE ASSOCIATES. "But the Staffords wouldn't sell their place."

"Oh, naturally not," Margaret said. "They're friends of mine. Camilla . . ."

"Yeah, I know Camilla, since we were kids. They're here every summer. When her mother was alive, all us kids used to go up there, but no more." He started to say more, then thought better of it. "It's easy to find," he said.

Indeed, it was a simple matter to locate the road to the Stafford house. On the way, she noticed that new houses had been built on the right-hand side of the main road, while the left remained almost entirely undeveloped. She turned onto Stafford Road, and then abruptly, she reached the end of the road and two stone pillars that marked the entrance to a drive. No gate barred her way, so she drove in and drove for a long way, closed in on either side by tall, thick trees that seemed undecided whether they were intended to be woods or parkland.

The Stafford house sat at the top of a low rise: brilliantly white stucco, four stories, with a porte cochere at the entrance and verandas all around, turrets and marble urns and the promise of grottoes and gardens and glassed-in conservatories. It was as though a French château had been wedded to an Italian Palladian villa and had produced a hybrid offspring that wasn't sure what it was, except that it was expensive. It spoke of a time when fortunes were recklessly spent on residences that were used but a few months a year.

A Jaguar and a long black Lincoln were parked on the broad gravel drive near a two-story garage suitable for a dozen autos. People were at home. Margaret would either have to drive away or brazen her way through in a ladylike manner. From the corner of her eye, she glimpsed a man in a gray uniform, likely the chauffeur, peering out at her from behind a ruthlessly clipped hedge. No turning back. Margaret rang the doorbell.

The sound echoed through the house and bounced back through open windows. Margaret detected the movement of a curtain at the window next to the front door.

"Hullo?" Margaret spoke toward the window.

Suddenly the door latch clicked and the door swung open slowly. A sturdy young woman in a maid's uniform looked at her suspiciously. "The Staffords are not at home," she said and started to close the door.

"So sorry to intrude," Margaret said. "I was passing through Cranford and wanted to catch a glimpse of the house. I've heard a great deal about it. I am," she said grandly with her best upper-class British intonation, "Lady Margaret Priam."

"I'll have to ask," the maid said. "Please wait." Margaret followed her inside. A vast hall lay before her, with marble floors and decorated ceilings. A huge chandelier, a regal double staircase, gilded curlicues, and even an immense tapestry on one wall. It imitated the great halls of the country houses of England where Margaret had grown up, but it did not quite succeed. It was a little too much the frenzied vision of some long-ago and very rich aspirer to architectural grandeur. It did not remind Margaret in the least of a comfortable summer home by the sea.

The maid said, "You'd better wait on the sun porch." Then she half smiled. "They call it something else—solarium, loggia, galleria, something—but at my house we'd call it a closed-in sun porch." She pointed off to the right where Margaret could see French doors at the end of a sort of drawing room. The maid hurried toward a closed door on the other side of the great hall.

Margaret went out to the solarium and startled another maid who was running a feather duster along a ledge. She scurried away into the house. It seemed totally peaceful. Not a sound from the house behind her, not a sound from outside. White wicker chairs and sofas were grouped here and there, with low tables displaying the mandatory issues of *Town & Country, House & Garden,* and *Harper's Bazaar*. There were shutters and bamboo blinds to shut off the chill or the darkness. There were huge baskets of artfully arranged summer flowers and tall palms in ceramic pots to fill the nooks and bring the outdoors inside.

It was the murder room shown in the old newspaper photo.

As Margaret waited, she seemed to hear a shrill voice carried by the breeze. The voice became a scream—rage or terror, Margaret could not tell. She looked through tall glass doors out onto a terrace and a pristine stretch of sloping lawn. To the sides and at the bottom of the lawn was a thick clustering of trees, and far out in the distance, a gleam of blue water: Long Island Sound. Ought she do something? Ought she pretend that she had heard nothing? The voice again, and this time she could understand words.

"Bastard," the voice shrieked. A woman. "I could kill you."

Margaret moved closer to the doors. She saw a lean

tanned woman emerging from the trees. She was running ahead of a solid-looking man in white shorts and shirt. He had thick, powerful thighs and arms. Not someone, Margaret thought, at whom one would casually hurl epithets. He overtook the woman, grabbed her arm, and swung her around. They engaged in what seemed to be a rather intense argument. Then they walked—quite calmly, it appeared—up the slope toward the far side of the house.

Margaret was about to withdraw so there would be no chance of being seen when she caught sight of a slight blond girl dressed in a long yellow sundress. She was peering out from behind an artistic jumble of rocks at the edge of the perfect lawn, observing the violent passage between the man and the woman.

"May I ask to whom I have the pleasure of speaking? The maid was unclear." A terribly refined woman's voice spoke behind Margaret. There was unmistakable steel in the sound: position, money, incalculable assurance.

"Awfully sorry." Margaret turned to face the woman. "I was admiring the view." From the corner of her eye, she saw that the man and the woman had disappeared. The girl had also vanished. The woman confronting her was regal and not at all amused. She was well past middle age but was expensively kept up, although not in the futilely glamorous way some older social ladies assayed. Margaret saw at once that she expected to be recognized as the epitome of Old Money and Old Family (or as old as American families can get). She was definitely not the housekeeper and could only be Eloise Stafford.

"I am Lady Margaret Priam," Margaret said. She chose to become regal in her turn. The Priam money and family were older by centuries. "I understand we are to lunch tomorrow, but in stopping at your lovely house, I had no idea I would actually intrude on you personally."

"Indeed," Eloise said, "it is no intrusion at all, Lady Margaret." She made an attempt at warmth. "I am delighted to make your acquaintance. I think we have not had the opportunity before. Lynne has told me of your extremely kind acceptance of her suggestion that you take poor Camilla in hand for the Season. I myself..." She fluttered a deprecating hand. "... am far too elderly to understand my granddaughter's generation. Although the *rules* of polite society are immutable, don't you think? One should be brought up knowing instinctively how one ought to behave. Poor Camilla was deprived of a mother's guidance. I've done my best, but I haven't been able to do much. She will benefit tremendously from her association with you."

Trapped, Margaret thought. "It will be my pleasure to ...um...work with Camilla," she said. Their dialogue seemed to come from a drawing room comedy of some decades past. "I absolutely had to see the house before we discussed our plans tomorrow. The first party, don't you know? To introduce Camilla early to some really nice young people. I wanted to be sure the house was suitable for informal entertaining. So many houses aren't, don't you find?" Margaret hated herself for sounding like an overbred snob, but she felt she had no choice under the circumstances.

"It's *most* suitable," Eloise said grandly. "How foresighted of you to think of it. We had superb parties here when I was a young woman. People simply flocked to us." Unspoken but implied: Very Important People. "My children choose to entertain in different ways." Margaret heard the disapproval.

"I should look about the grounds," Margaret said.

"What a pity that I have to leave almost at once for a pressing engagement. Perhaps you wouldn't mind looking about on your own," Eloise Stafford said.

"Not at all." Margaret oozed graciousness. "And I was hoping to speak with Camilla."

"Not at home," Eloise said quickly. "She is staying down in the village with one of her little local summer friends. Donna Kessler..." Eloise paused. "A nice enough girl. We know the family. The father is a local businessman."

"Real estate, is it?" Margaret asked casually.

"Yes," Eloise said shortly. "Tomorrow will be soon

enough for you to meet Camilla." She looked at her Cartier watch, then took a small notebook and a gold pen from the pocket of her sensible but extremely well-made print skirt. She made a note. "I will see you tomorrow at one at the house in the city. We will eat in, since the cook is there without a thing to do most of the time. I must be on my way. My chauffeur becomes nervous if he has to drive too fast."

"Don't let me delay you," Margaret said. "I'll just walk around the grounds."

"If you walk down the lawn, you'll find a path down the hill to the inlet from the Sound. The young people go swimming there when the tide's in. When you circle the house, you'll see the gardens. My late husband was fond of gardens. The old stables have been turned into the guest house. The children's playhouse that was built long ago for my husband's sisters is closed up. Camilla was never a child to play house. But you will find her delightful."

Margaret waited until Eloise had disappeared into the house. Then she headed toward the clump of rocks where she had seen the girl who was probably Camilla.

Margaret had not gone far before she was face-to-face with the couple she had seen earlier. They appeared quite relaxed, although the man grasped his companion's darkly tanned arm.

The woman said brightly, "Lady Margaret Priam, isn't it? I'm Nancy Stafford. We've met."

"We might have done," Margaret said cautiously, "although I can't recall. . . ."

"It was Martha Pelham's or someplace like that. I can't bear her, but one of her husbands was terribly attractive. I can't tell you what a relief it is that you're taking Camilla in hand." News traveled fast in Stafford family circles. Nancy made no move to introduce her escort, nor did he choose to make himself known. He merely scowled at a point beyond Margaret. Up close, he was almost good-looking in a hard, slick sort of way, the kind of assured male that dismisses women talking as irrelevant. He did not look as though he had spent his youth sipping tea and attending dancing classes in white gloves. Margaret imagined that Eloise loathed the sight of him.

"Naturally I'll do anything I can, if my schedule permits," Nancy said. "I just *adore* Camilla, poor baby. She's had such tragedy in her life. You know about my sister-in-law's murder. . . ."

Margaret was surprised to hear it mentioned, but she suspected that Nancy's tongue knew few restraints.

"We have to go now," the man said. His grip on her arm tightened. Margaret now saw a bruise on Nancy's cheek, another on her arm. Her gentleman friend was not gentle.

"So nice to have seen you," Nancy said mechanically. "We'll meet this evening for cocktails?"

"No, no," Margaret said hastily. "I'll be heading back to New York shortly."

"You *must* stay. Mother and I are here *all* alone. Daniel's in Manhattan and might not come up tonight. My brother Toby used to spend all his summers here, but these days he says he's too busy to rot in the sun like an overripe orange." She almost pouted. "He used to be such fun. The tennis courts are simply going to waste."

"Come on," the man said.

"Richie, we don't want to be rude to Lady Margaret. She's doing us a tremendous favor." The now-named Richie looked directly at Margaret. He appeared to be deriving considerable enjoyment from being rude. "We'll meet again in New York, then," Nancy said. "Why don't we have lunch one day soon."

Margaret said, "Let's do," intending never to do so. "Awfully nice to run into you. I think I'll just stroll down toward the water."

"It's quite nice on the beach. I do prefer the ocean to the pool Daniel insisted we install. Until . . ." Nancy waved gaily, as though she and Richie didn't have a care in the world.

Margaret proceeded toward the water and did not look back.

The girl in the long dress was sitting on a mossy patch, leaning against a tall tree, and staring down toward the tiny beach at the bottom of the path. She could be quite pretty, Margaret thought, if she would take the trouble. She looked very young; not at all like the self-assured debs Margaret had encountered during her few years in New York.

"You're Camilla," Margaret said softly.

The girl wasn't startled. She turned her head calmly to squint up at Margaret, surveying her with a look that could only be called hostile.

"Yes."

"My name is Lady Margaret Priam," she said.

"Delighted to meet you. How lovely of you to stop by. Isn't it a heavenly day?" Camilla spoke like a perfect little prep school princess. Margaret thought it was a rather elaborate pose. "One of Aunt Nancy's friends? Or one of Daddy's?"

"Neither," Margaret said. "Your aunt Lynne and your grandmother asked me—"

Camilla flung back her head and gazed up through the branches of the tree. "It's the debut, right?"

"Right."

"Dear Lady Whoever." Camilla enunciated the words slowly and clearly. "I do not want to be a debutante. I do not want to meet a fine young man from Yale to marry. I do not want to go to college at Brown or Smith or Wellesley. I don't want to go to parties and have pretty little dresses. I just want to go far away. Daddy says I'm not old enough to be on my own yet, so I'm stuck here." She shrugged. "What am I supposed to do?"

"What would you do if you went far away?"

Camilla hesitated. "Nothing. Well, I'd work."

Margaret almost laughed but was glad she didn't. "Work isn't what they say it is," she said. "It's not always fun."

"My girlfriend works in her father's real estate office part-time. She has fun." Camilla shrugged. "I'd like to help poor people, or take care of babies who didn't have anyone to love them." She stood up. "I don't want to come out in society."

"We're supposed to be meeting for lunch tomorrow in

New York to discuss turning you into a debutante. That's something your family wants you to do, and sometimes we have to do what our families want."

Camilla defiantly refused to meet Margaret's eye.

"If you decide to go along with the idea," Margaret said, "I'll help you. If you don't, please understand that I don't care."

"Hey, okay. Don't get upset." Camilla stood up. "I'll be nice at lunch. But please don't say you saw me today." She sounded uneasy.

"Whatever you wish," Margaret said.

"I'm not supposed to be here. I told Grandmummy that I'd be with my friend Donna Kessler today, but I wanted to get something I'd forgotten. They always like to know where I am. They don't like me talking to strangers."

"I'm not exactly a stranger," Margaret said.

"They worry, I guess. Ever since my mother was killed—" She stopped. "Did you know she was murdered here?" Camilla stopped and stared away over the trees. "Four years ago this summer."

"I had heard something. You don't need to talk about it." Margaret was dying to hear, and she was dying to ask about the servants. And since everybody seemed willing to mention the murder, she might have the opportunity.

"It was awful." Camilla began to speak as though she were repeating a well-memorized fairy tale. "I was in the village with Donna Kessler and some kids, and it was time to go home so I came up through the woods. There was no one in the house, no one at all, and then I found her." She stopped. "In the solarium."

"I wondered that she would be in this big house all alone—with none of the servants about to hear the intruder."

Camilla jerked her head around and stared at Margaret. It was a defiant look, daring Margaret to deny the truth of what she'd said. "That's how it was. The servants were all gone for the day. Grandmummy gave some of them the day off, and the rest of them were off doing things for Daddy or Uncle Toby. Aunt Nancy says servants are unreliable, always sneaking off when nobody's watching. They all left us after it happened, except Grandmummy's driver. Daddy took me to Europe, and Uncle Toby went with us for a while, but that's when he started putting his jazz group together. Aunt Lynne wanted to come, too, but Daddy said no."

"I'm terribly sorry," Margaret said.

"Grandmummy says one oughtn't discuss such things as murder." The contrived prep school voice. "One can afford to ignore bad things if one is rich." Camilla suddenly looked downcast. "We're very rich, you know, me especially, because of the way my grandfather fixed the trusts."

"It hadn't occurred to me," Margaret murmured, "that you would be quite rich."

"I don't have the money yet because of the trusts." Camilla had a funny, secret smile. "I have to be older first. Uncle Toby says we ought to give our money away to poor people. He says money is wicked." She almost grinned. "But he still has this really great apartment in the Village and his club, which isn't so hot. Aunt Nancy thinks money is terrific, but she's crazy. I mean, a guy like Richie . . ." Camilla shuddered. "One time I had to bite him. You know." Camilla was grandly disgusted at the thought of Richie.

"I think I do," Margaret said and knew that if she suspected Richie was even thinking about touching her, she would bite him, too.

"I have to keep out of the way until later," Camilla said. "Otherwise I'll have to play tennis with Aunt Nancy. Promise not to say anything tomorrow." She looked at Margaret anxiously and was reassured. Then she slipped down the path and ran across the beach. Margaret glimpsed her ducking into the trees that crowded the beach just above the high tide line, and she disappeared.

"I should not be involved in this," Margaret said aloud to the clean, expensive air above and around Cranford, Connecticut. "These are not savory people." But then she looked toward the house with its elegant solarium and shining windows, its neat sloping lawn and the huge old trees. A perfect setting for a party with lights and music and tents. Long, old-fashioned dresses for the girls and white jackets for the boys. Camilla with her hair done just right wearing a pretty white frock embroidered with pink and blue and yellow flowers. A thousand silver balloons floating above the party on colored strings. Violins perhaps. Fireworks to end the evening. Very romantic.

Margaret started to walk back to the drive where she had left her car. The house loomed large and white in the midday sun. It was hard to believe that four years ago, someone had crept along the winding drive close to the trees, intent on robbery and confident that no one, not even the servants, would be at home. And finding someone— Ann Stafford—why would he bother to stab and hack and bludgeon instead of escaping?

She stopped. There was definitely more to Ann Stafford's murder than people cared to admit. She decided to ask the one person who might know something.

Matt Kessler, of Cranford Real Estate Associates, was tanned and fortyish, in white slacks and a washed denim shirt begat by Ralph Lauren. He looked as though he used to wear at least one gold chain.

"I'm Margaret Priam. I'm up from New York looking at a house," Margaret began, not quite truthfully.

"You've come to the right place for houses," Kessler said. He liked to talk. Margaret let him talk on. "You're English, right? Great people, the English. I handle almost everything around here that comes on the market. As a matter of fact, I have a few prime lots left in Cranford Hills, a little development I put together. If you build, you get what you want."

"Where would Cranford Hills be?"

"You know the town? It's up on the other side of Stafford Road, beyond the Stafford estate. Important family, one of the last of the old timers left in town."

"I've met some Staffords," Margaret said cautiously.

"Yes, you would know them. I've known them for

years. Toby Stafford was a pal when we were growing up. Great guy. My kid's a friend of the Stafford girl. In fact, my development is on land the Staffords used to own."

"I didn't imagine they were the kind to sell off land."

"Three, four years back, old Mrs. Stafford—Eloise Stafford—fixed it so I'd have first refusal on any Stafford property that came on the market. Keep it in the town, you know. A couple years ago, the family decided to sell off a piece at the far end of the estate. I've done pretty well with the development. Country living close to the city. I could give you a good price on one of the remaining lots." He imagined his gleaming smile was very, very sexy. She did not need another randy suburban husband sniffing at her heels, although Matt Kessler was a fairly good-looking example of the type.

Margaret took a deep breath. "Would your fortunate business relationship with Mrs. Stafford have anything to do with the fact that your daughter was with Camilla the day her mother was murdered?"

Matt Kessler turned hostile. "If you're a newspaper type poking around about the Stafford murder, you can forget it."

"I'm not a newspaper person. I'm a friend of the family. They asked me to do them a favor, and I need . . ." She decided to make him helpless to resist the fact that she *needed* him. "I need to know from someone I can trust exactly what happened. I was hoping to speak with your daughter." Margaret did not believe for a second that Matt Kessler would permit it, but it never hurt to try. "I've heard different things from different people."

"What 'people'?"

"Some say it was someone Ann Stafford knew. Someone else said Camilla was actually there when it happened. I don't know what to believe," Margaret said. "Camilla is so young and confused." She leaned toward him with an intimate smile. "I do need your help."

Matt Kessler sat down in the big leather chair behind his desk and looked to be a man composing a suitable story rather than preparing to speak the whole truth. "I liked Ann

Stafford, and it was a terrible thing to have happen. But get out of your mind any idea that there's a connection between that land and the murder. Things got tight financially for the Staffords a couple years ago, and they needed cash. Dan came to me with the land proposition, and I went for it. Nobody ever said a word about the murder. As for what happened, Donna told me what everybody knows. Camilla went home and found her mother dead."

"What about Donna's mother? Would Donna or Camilla have confided in her?"

"Donna's mother left me not long before Ann's murder," he said shortly. "I only remarried two years ago. I don't think Donna would talk about it with her stepmother anyhow, although they get along well enough."

"What was Ann Stafford like?"

"A nice woman," Matt said. "Out of her element. She was an ordinary middle class person who happened to be very beautiful. I don't know how she lasted that long with the Staffords, who have a very grand view of themselves. Ann did a lot of the social things, but she wasn't happy about it. Most of the family never thought she was good enough for Dan. I thought it was the other way around."

"Did she have lovers?"

Matt looked at her sharply. "That's none of my business, and none of yours." He stood up.

Margaret decided not to end the conversation quite yet. "About Camilla. Is she all right now?"

"Funny kid," Matt said. "She talked Donna into running away to New York, after Dan brought her back from Europe. You don't know what kids are going to learn over there. We found them pronto before they ended up as teenage hookers. Donna's a sensible kid. Likes her comforts. She was on the next train home. The Staffords retrieved Camilla undamaged from Toby's place."

"I'm supposed to be helping Camilla with her debut," Margaret said. "That's really what this is all about."

Matt shook his head. "Donna's been talking about that. It's too high class for the likes of us, but if Camilla wants Donna to go along for the ride, I'll spring for what she needs. Donna loves the idea. Wishes we were society folk. Wishes we were as rich as the Staffords." He paused. "As rich as they claim to be." Matt Kessler seemed to feel he had said enough or possibly too much. He escorted her out to the street. "Are you sure I can't show you some property?"

"I'm not in the market for a house right now," Margaret said, "but if I ever am . . ."

She was distracted by the sight of a silver Mercedes convertible racing past, with an unmistakable Daniel Stafford at the wheel. Back from New York in the middle of the day. Nancy would be pleased.

"You know him?" Matt asked. He did not sound as though Dan was his greatest friend on the entire East Coast.

"Only in passing," Margaret said. The Mercedes turned at the corner and headed toward Stafford Road. A remarkably attractive man was Daniel Stafford.

"Poor Ann," Matt said. "Between Eloise and Nancy, not to mention that hard bitch of a sister who's still after Dan, she never had a chance. She tried, though. Maybe if they'd had more kids, it would have worked out differently, but by the time I got to know her well, she'd had it with Dan and the Stafford life."

A glimmer of an idea edged into her mind: Matt Kessler had once been on much more intimate terms with Ann Stafford than he cared to let on.

Another thought: Was Camilla resisting her debut because the social life of the Staffords had brought only tragedy to her mother? Or had her mother influenced her against the trappings of society that the grandmother so much wanted her to wear?

Very bad business, Margaret thought, but let's first see how we all behave tomorrow at lunch.

Chapter 4

After the fact, Margaret concluded that the Staffords did not behave at all well.

Margaret had arrived at the Stafford's New York address at one and found herself looking up at four stories of Federal townhouse, all rosy brick and white trim. Neat window boxes, trimmed boxwood shrubs in the small courtyard off the street, polished brass fixtures on the heavy dark door. Very nice, she thought, and very expensive real estate. She herself spent far too much of her resources just to keep a modest Manhattan roof over her head.

Then a manservant was opening the door and leading Margaret into a swirl of pleasantly chilled air, and thence to a serene drawing room in beiges and geranium, more masculine than feminine, more Daniel probably than his late wife or one of the other Stafford females. Margaret caught sight of a private, shady city garden at the back of the house, with well-tended borders and ornamental trees and ivy covering the brick walls of adjacent buildings.

"Lady Margaret, what a pleasure to see you again. It's been too long." Daniel Stafford exuded waves of charm. "Mother and Camilla will join us shortly. Some little difference of opinion on what to wear."

"Mr. Stafford, I truthfully can't recall where we met."

"Daniel, please." He guided her to a chair, he smiled, he glowed with high-priced male grooming products and worldly ease.

He laughed. "I don't remember myself. I'll ring for sherry, shall I?" And rang before she could speak. The manservant appeared immediately with a tray, glasses, and a sherry decanter. "Lynne Jordan tells me that you and she share a long and close friendship."

"I know her in the way one does, but I can't claim... intimacy."

"I see. Lynne has a remarkably vivid imagination for one with so few pretensions to intellect. Because of my late wife, we continue to feel an obligation..." He did not sound pleased.

"You have a lovely house," Margaret said, to fill the awkward silence that ensued.

"My mother's doing," Daniel said, "and my sister Nancy's when she isn't engaged on some matrimonial escapade. I try to give Camilla a happy home."

"Your wife didn't live here, then?"

"We lived elsewhere when she was alive," he said. "You will have heard of our tragedy."

"Lynne mentioned something," Margaret said carefully.

"She does enjoy sharing information," Daniel said. He sipped his sherry and spoke to the air. "I wanted to see you alone, before lunch, to speak about Camilla. She was always a stubborn little thing, but since Ann's death, she's been very difficult. I spend as much time with her as I can." He gazed soulfully at Margaret. "I am deeply concerned. It's hard to grow up without a mother's guidance." Evidently Daniel did not think of Lynne Jordan as an adequate mother substitute. "My mother feels that if she becomes a part of a lively circle of young people, she'll gain a different perspective."

"I am not altogether sure I will be able to turn Camilla's life around. I don't even know her." That she had met Camilla was surely different from knowing her.

Daniel continued. "We feel that if Camilla were involved with young men of good family and girls who are into the swing of youthful New York life, she'd put aside some foolish notions she has."

"Doesn't she attend school, then?"

"She has," Daniel said. "Farmington for a year, but she didn't care for it. She attended Cranford High School for a bit, but Mother didn't think it appropriate. She's tried some schools here in Manhattan. . . ." He shrugged ruefully: Who can understand teenage girls? "This last year she has been tutored here at home."

Margaret did not know a great deal about the educational system in the United States, but she could not but feel that Camilla had been given short shrift when it came to educational opportunities.

"She's highly intelligent," Daniel said. "It runs in the family. Both Nancy and I did very well in college while we were there. Even my brother Toby."

What an insufferable prig, Margaret thought.

"Ah, Mother, and Camilla darling."

Eloise had put aside her country/casual clothes and had become a cross between the Queen Mother and the pride of the mature woman's department at Saks. Camilla looked demure in a little blue suit and low-heeled shoes.

"Lady Margaret, I know you've met my mother, but here is my little Camilla."

"Lovely to meet you," Margaret said to Camilla. "At last," she added meaningfully.

Camilla smiled faintly. "How do you do?" she said. "I have been looking forward to meeting you ever since Grandmummy told me you had agreed to help with my debut. Won't it be fun?"

Margaret noted the monotone tinged with sarcasm.

"I'm sure we will have a wonderful time," Margaret said.

"Shall we go in to lunch?" Eloise was already leading the way. "We have a good deal to discuss. Daniel will be joining us, Lady Margaret. He wants so much to participate in this important stage of Camilla's life."

Margaret enjoyed a superb lunch (of course), and did not fail to observe that each Stafford had memorized his/ her excruciatingly polite lines very well indeed. Daniel and Eloise seemed in no rush to discuss the debut. Rather they were intent on impressing Margaret with their connections, good breeding, wealth, and general prominence in the social scheme of things. Camilla ate silently, scarcely looking at her father and grandmother.

Finally Eloise said, "Daniel, did I mention that Lády Margaret has cleverly suggested a party at the Cranford house to introduce Camilla to some new young people, as well as the children of our friends? When did you propose to hold it?"

"Soon," Margaret said. "Perhaps around the beginning of September. The young people will be back from Europe and won't yet have started to return to school. The weather will still be quite nice. . . ."

Margaret rattled off her plans, with inward thanks to her friend Dianne Stark, a former airline attendant who had married well into New York society. Dianne had explained to Margaret a few of the intricacies of the debutante scene and gave warning: "The kids aren't so bad, but the parents —whee! The nouvelle society types can be as mean as they come, and the Old Guard are too grand for words, but in the end, all it takes is money. Lucky you have a title. Use it for all it's worth."

"I'm afraid it will not be inexpensive," Margaret said, in the hope that this would discourage the Staffords and she might withdraw gracefully.

Alas, the money part was easy. "I've already arranged for a checking account," Daniel said. "I will need your signature for the bank. You have carte blanche."

"Really?" Margaret said. "How curious. Should I wish to purchase a yacht or a diamond necklace or a house in the Hamptons . . ."

Daniel laughed. "How amusing. Shall we say, within reason? And whatever you will need for the Cotillion and so forth this winter."

"I haven't precisely agreed to do much beyond the September party," Margaret said. "It may not work out."

"But it will," Eloise said. "You—and Daniel—must make this the loveliest time in Camilla's young life." Camilla glowered at her grandmother and picked at her raspberries and cream. "And in return, Camilla will behave like

the young lady we have brought her up to be, conscious
that the world looks up to the Staffords."

Margaret thought Camilla's dainty cough masked a
strangled shriek of laughter.

Eloise droned on. "All the sadness will vanish, and Camilla will be on her way to a lovely future—"

"And the Stafford name will shine again with the reflected glory of unearned and highly tainted wealth." The
man at the dining room door was bearded and comfortably
shabby, but Margaret was quick to notice that it was cus-
tom-tailored shabbiness.

"Uncle Toby!" Camilla sprang from her chair and threw
herself at him.

"Camilla, behave yourself. Toby, Toby, why must you
always appear when you are least needed, and never when
we do want you?"

"Thank you, Mother, for your kind support. How's it
going, Dan? Still frittering away the family fortune and
terrorizing the help?"

"I've been trying to reach you, Toby. I need your signature on some documents," Daniel said sharply. "Lady Margaret, this is my younger brother Toby Stafford."

"Lady Margaret, you say? What ho! Or is it 'Tally ho'?"

"You are impossible, Toby," Eloise said. "This is Lady
Margaret Priam, a dear friend of ours who's agreed to assist in Camilla's debut. Camilla, do stop clinging and sit
down. We haven't finished our lunch."

"Lunch sounds fine," Toby said and pulled a chair to the
table. The manservant appeared swiftly, followed by a
maid. A place was set before Toby; his lunch was placed in
front of him.

"How is it you happen to be here?" Daniel asked.

"Family grapevine," Toby said.

"Thank goodness, I'm not late!" Lynne Jordan rushed
into the dining room. "Eloise darling, I do apologize for
bursting in on you, but I simply had to know how matters
were proceeding. Hello, Dan. I had no idea you'd be
here." She blew him a dainty kiss with her still perfectly
manicured hand. "And Toby, what an absolute treat."

Toby honored her with a baleful look.

"Lynne, dear. How nice of you to drop in." Eloise's mouth was a tight line. "Please do sit down with us. Lunch?"

"I've lunched," she said. "Perrier and lime," she said over her shoulder to the hovering maid.

"Vodka and tonic for me, lots of lime." Nancy Stafford's arrival made the party complete. "Both my lovely siblings in one place. And Lynne, too. Isn't this a surprise!"

"Are you alone?" Eloise asked ominously.

"Richie is off buying whatever guys buy when they get to New York City. Is that who you mean, Mother?"

"It was," Eloise said.

"Camilla baby, aren't you excited?" Nancy hugged Camilla from behind, who stoically submitted. "I had such a mingy little debut at our old house on Sixty-seventh Street. But this one is going to be great fun for all of us." Then, with a nod to Eloise: "But perhaps not like the extravaganza that introduced you to society, Mother."

Camilla said in a surprisingly calm and mature voice, "You all know that I have no interest in a debut. I don't know why you think it will be fun for me, but perhaps you will enjoy spending a lot of money that could do good elsewhere."

Daniel leaned toward Margaret. "Pay no attention. She's been influenced by Toby and his mad ideas."

"I'll go through with it," Camilla continued, "but only if Lady Margaret does it with me. If she won't, I won't." Camilla's glance flickered toward Margaret, then quickly away.

Why, she trusts me, Margaret thought, because I didn't say that I'd seen her yesterday at Cranford. She doesn't trust her family one bit. Margaret's thoughts raced. Is there something she knows? Did she see something four years ago?

Then Margaret told herself to stop it. If there were anything to be known, a frightened young girl would have told someone. She looked around the table at the Staffords. Perhaps she had.

"Camilla," Eloise said, "you and I have come to an understanding, and I expect you to keep your end of the bargain."

"Of course I'll do it," Margaret said quickly.

"Thank you," Daniel said. Margaret did not miss the peculiar look from Lynne as Daniel placed his hand briefly on Margaret's. Nor did she miss Eloise's pleased expression at the same gesture. Or Nancy's near smirk as she downed her vodka and tonic and gestured for another.

"Daniel tells me you've already made local Cranford acquaintances," Nancy said somewhat archly. "He saw you speaking to the Kessler man in Cranford Center."

They were all watching Margaret.

"Do you refer to the real estate man?" Margaret asked warily.

Toby broke the tension. "Good old Matt. Quite the ladies' man. Always has been. Remember, Dan, how the three of us guys used to chase bikinis at the yacht club in the old days?"

"The Kesslers have never been members of the yacht club," Eloise said. "Nice enough people, but—"

"Not like us," Toby finished. "Margaret, Lady Something, since you are like us, and almost a member of the family, you've got to hear my group play."

"You *must* hear," Eloise said under her breath, a correction rather than a word of support.

"For all his flaws," Nancy said, "he's a pretty good musician. We'll go, next week perhaps. Just us two girls."

"We'll all go," Daniel said, rather too heartily.

"Curiously, I'm free and in the city all next week," Lynne said, belying her fervent desire to get out of town. She remembered suddenly and added, "Tiresome legal business."

"Picking up the alimony check?" Toby said. "You'll bleed poor old Philip dry. He's probably dying for you to remarry."

"I'd love to hear your group, Toby," Margaret said. She felt a twinge of resentment that the Staffords had put her in the position of family peacemaker, when she scarcely knew them. "Please do give me the particulars of time and place, and I'll try to drop in. If I'm free."

Eloise stood up suddenly. Lunch was over, although the latecomers were not yet finished.

Margaret signed a signature card for a checking account that would allow her to spend up to twenty thousand dollars for the party in early September at the Cranford estate. Daniel quietly handed her a check for five thousand dollars, "for your initial trouble."

"My brother and I and Matt Kessler did do a little girl-chasing when we were younger," he said unexpectedly. "What did you think of him?"

"Think? Nothing at all. I had an impulsive query about property in the area."

"Mother said you'd mentioned his name at the house."

"I?" Margaret signed her name with a flourish. "I believe your mother mentioned him to me."

She had time alone with Camilla only to suggest they meet soon to talk about the party. "Come to my apartment, if you like," Margaret said. "We'll go over all the plans."

"They wouldn't like that. Grandmummy likes discussions on her own ground," Camilla said.

"It's not Grandmummy's party, it's yours."

"I guess I could think of a way," Camilla said slowly. "I'll let you know—"

"Camilla dear," Eloise interrupted effectively.

"Lady Margaret has such perfectly lovely ideas," Camilla said brightly. "It will be fun. So nice to meet you." Camilla didn't quite curtsy. Margaret admired her dramatic abilities.

When Margaret had walked the half block to the corner to catch an uptown cab, Toby Stafford was waiting.

"My lucky guess," he said. "I figured you'd go uptown rather than down."

"Yes, very lucky. What can I do for you?"

"You can not do it. The debut. Get out of it. Better yet, stop it. It isn't going to turn Camilla's life around. She needs to escape, not be drawn further into this life."

Margaret looked at Toby. Beneath the careless surface, he shared his brother's attractiveness. Margaret supposed he must be wealthy, like the rest of the family. If, as had been implied, he felt uncomfortable about his unearned wealth, that was understandable. Margaret had encountered a number of heirs to American fortunes who were guilt-ridden about the money thrust upon them and made ill-conceived attempts to dispose of it to the less well-endowed.

"Her father and Mrs. Stafford seem to want this," Margaret said. "There is the good argument that if I refused to do it, they would hire someone else."

Toby laughed cynically. "Believe me, they've tried. None of the top women who make a good living bringing out debs will touch Camilla. The lesser ones wouldn't do my mother the kind of good she needs."

"Clout," Margaret murmured.

"Exactly," Toby said. "The family needs all it can get to cover over some of our sins. And you . . ." He stepped back and squinted at her. "I imagine my mother sees you and Daniel finding bliss as you work side by side for the good of his unhappy daughter. Mother would like grandsons to carry on the Stafford name. I'm a bad bet and my sister is impossible. Of course, Mother would be pleased to marry Camilla off to some wealthy but witless scion of a good family. Preferably from very far out of town. They feel guilty every time they look at her."

"Guilty?"

"The family is to blame for her mother's death. If she hadn't been there, at that time and place—but of course she had to be."

"Do you feel guilty, too?"

"I'm beyond all that," Toby said. "Besides, I didn't have anything to do with bringing her into the Stafford family, with its money and social pretensions. I didn't make her unhappy."

Margaret wasn't sure he was telling the absolute truth. There was a shifty look to him.

"Tell me more about Ann. About the murder."

"We don't speak of Ann's murder," Toby said. "I don't, anyhow. Ann had a good life handed to her, and she lost it. She was the ideal victim."

"To be murdered by an intruder?"

"To have a circle of circumstances get smaller and smaller, until there wasn't anything left to do but die."

"I don't understand."

"Look, it was some nut robbing the house, and Ann got in the way." He was no longer quite so amiable. "Don't forget to come hear my group." He turned on his heel and walked briskly downtown without a glance back.

Margaret went home to ponder what she had gotten herself into.

Her hard-working answering machine was full of surprises: Prince Paul Castrocani was back in New York and wanted her to dine with him that evening.

More long-distance friends were beginning to find life on the beaches and in the cool mountains was not quite so nice without Margaret. They had left pleading messages for her to visit.

Nancy Stafford had left a message immediately after lunch, while Margaret was still making her way home. An invitation to a Bridgehampton weekend. Margaret would definitely not accept.

A real surprise: Daniel. In his brief message, he regretted that he had neglected to speak of it at lunch, but would she join him for dinner one day next week when she was free?

Then the phone rang and it was Camilla.

"Can you come to Connecticut on Friday? Everyone will be away except a couple of the maids, and they won't say anything. We can talk without the grownups."

"I'll be there," Margaret said. Then she looked at herself in the mirror above the phone and was flattered that to one young human being, she was not lumped with the grownups. Grownups were coercive, unfriendly, manipulative. Possibly murderous. But Margaret was possibly a friend.

Then she looked again and wondered whether she was

seriously being considered as a potential breeder of Stafford sons. She would graciously but firmly put a stop to that.

She telephoned Paul and made dinner arrangements. He was pleased. A nice young man, Margaret thought, who deserved to win the heart of a beautiful heiress. A pity Camilla was too young for him, just as Margaret was a decade too old (and merely comfortable, not extremely rich).

Then she took a long bath in bubbles and pondered why she was suddenly so extraordinarily popular with the Staffords. Since lunch, only Eloise and Lynne had failed to extend the hand of friendship. But Margaret had pondered too soon. Eloise's flowers arrived by messenger; Lynne called to beg for another lunch soon.

"Such a delight to be working with you," Lynne said.

Margaret decided not to mention that the whole point of seducing Margaret into the debut was to free Lynne. Perhaps Daniel's attentions to Margaret had altered her attitude. Margaret promised to find time for lunch someday soon.

Margaret decided to make mental lists of what extravagances she might buy for herself with the Staffords' five thousand dollars.

Chapter 5

"*No, they* did not behave at all well," Margaret told Paul that evening. "I managed to remain thoroughly civilized. How nice that you're back in New York so soon."

On the very morning Margaret had driven to Cranford for her initial close encounter with the Staffords, Paul Castrocani had surrendered to a reasonable impulse to escape Dallas and his mother's efforts to involve him in a tawdry liaison with a blue-eyed Texas beauty who was as hard as her hairspray. Not that New York was his city of choice by any means, but it was where he worked at United National Bank and Trust at the command of his stepfather, Benton Hoopes.

Margaret and Paul were dining at a newly opened imitation brasserie in Paul's Chelsea neighborhood, a location again not of his choice; his mother owned the small apartment building where he lived rent-free. Carolyn Sue Dennis Castrocani Hoopes kept a well-tended finger in many a financial and real estate pie.

The brasserie had food that was not at all bad, although the ambience was resolutely trendy. The waiters, fledgling actors awaiting The Call, recited complicated specials that Margaret could not recall by the end of the speech. The wine list was demandingly long with, as Paul noted, really very few fine choices and those grossly overpriced.

He chose a *Chianti classico*. "I know the man who owns the vineyard," he said. "He has a *fantastico* Maserati to support as well as a truly glorious mistress. She once told me with regret that she found me too young but would

47

entertain thoughts of me in a decade or so. I don't believe a man can be too young—"

"Pay attention, dear Paul," Margaret said. "I must ask you about these Staffords."

"But I must relax for a moment in this great city which is the gateway to my various homelands, as Dallas is not. Did you know that De Vere seems to be in town? I have not yet seen him."

"I had heard," Margaret said shortly. "It doesn't matter, until he is free to see me."

It did matter a little though, and even Paul knew this. He knew a good deal, since he shared his duplex apartment with Detective De Vere. Paul seldom did anything grossly illegal, and De Vere kept radically different hours, so the arrangement worked well. So far.

Paul was aware, for example, that Margaret and De Vere's was a delicate relationship, hovering at the brink of being serious. Their lives often took them in wildly different directions, and there were long stretches when there might be nothing more than a late-night phone call to Margaret from De Vere. Margaret even wondered aloud to Paul whether De Vere might have a girlfriend, in spite of the attentions he paid her. Paul always said he knew nothing, although he privately thought that two or three attractive women were only just ample for a reasonably young man like De Vere.

"What do you know about odd families?" Margaret said as wine was poured. "American crazy, as opposed to our dotty old European aristocrats who run about naked on the ski slopes or lie down to be trampled by the hunt to protect a fox."

"I know only what I observe," Paul said. "My father's side of the family is quite sane, although European and aristocratic. I would not say my mother is crazy, although American and obsessed by a need for possessions—I am grateful that they include real estate. In any event, you know Carolyn Sue."

"I am thinking specifically about the Staffords."

"I am acquainted with Daniel Stafford," Paul said. "I

have met him at the Vertical Club, where I sometimes work out."

"Definitely a member of the family. There was a murder, Daniel Stafford's wife."

Paul said sternly, "That murder is now and again mentioned. However, I believe I have made it clear in the past that I do not wish to be concerned with murder."

"Oh, you won't be, nor will I. Exactly."

"Then why are you speaking of it?"

"I had lunch the other day with Lynne Jordan. . . ."

"Ah . . ."

"You know her?"

"On one occasion she indicated that she did not find me too young, but I did not find her to my taste. She seemed to wear the disguise of a certain class rather than to be authentic."

"Lynne is the aunt of Camilla Stafford, and she wanted me to assist Camilla in making her debut this winter."

Paul was gazing into the space above Margaret's head where the dark green walls and the polished wood and brass attempted to convey the homey comforts of a bistro in the heart of Paris.

"I have not heard of Camilla Stafford," Paul said. "Perhaps she is too young for my circle."

"Let me tell you about today."

She told him as they ate wilted lettuce with hot bacon and delicately broiled scallops and perfect strawberry tart. From where Paul was seated, he could give an ear to Margaret but still keep a close eye on an exceptionally beautiful young woman in a rather small white dress who was dining with an expensively kept-up older man.

"And I do find the murderous intruder a bit difficult to believe," Margaret concluded.

"Margaret," Paul said sternly. "I understand that you believe something has been hidden about this murder."

"No one was ever arrested, but Camilla might have seen—"

Paul raised his hand. "*Silenzio!* If something has been

hidden, I am saying that you do not wish to discover it. I speak from experience. And so does he."

Paul's fine Roman profile was no longer turned toward the young lovely but toward the entrance to the restaurant.

"De Vere," Margaret said. "How did he find us, if it is us he is seeking?"

Paul shrugged. "It is simple. I left a note at the apartment telling him where we would be."

"So, you told him." Margaret was quite pleased. "But we should not say a word about—"

"Murder," Paul said "Naturally not. He pays his rent to me, not my mother, and I cannot afford to agitate him."

There was a moment just before De Vere borrowed a chair from an empty table to share a corner of theirs that Margaret thought he might bend to kiss her cheek, but he merely laid a hand briefly on her shoulder.

"I didn't expect to see you so soon," she said.

"I had a couple of hours free," De Vere said. "I'm looking into matters that aren't nice, but you two are. It's good to see you, Margaret." He looked away from her to Paul. "How is Carolyn Sue?"

"My mother remains much as you remember her," Paul said. "She has undertaken to build an extension to the Hoopes mansion to house her clothes. I understand there will be a climate-controlled room for her fur coats so they will feel as though they are still small furry animals in the wild. I could live comfortably for two years on what she pays for the construction. She asked to be remembered to—y'all."

"My mother," De Vere said, "is quite different from yours in both style and substance, yet I believe the two share certain common ground. A feeling for family, in spite of what their sons have chosen as their life's work."

"I have not chosen to work at United National Bank and Trust," Paul said glumly. "My stepfather chose it. He does not understand how weak my addition and multiplication are, even with the aid of a calculator."

"What you would choose, then?" De Vere said and laughed.

"I have chosen," Paul said, "but it costs more money than I possess to be an idle man about the city. About the world."

"I can't remember when I chose to be a policeman," De Vere said. "There are days now when I wish I had chosen something else. Paul, do you mind if I take Margaret away?" he said suddenly. "I'd like to get the thought of savage murders and sad people out of my mind for a while."

Margaret looked at Paul quickly and found him gazing at the departure of the luscious young thing across the way, who was a touch older and wiser than she had first appeared.

"I'd like that," Margaret said. "Paul can usually take care of himself. Paul, I will see you in two days, then."

Paul blinked but did not question an appointment he had not made.

De Vere stood up and edged toward the exit.

Paul whispered quickly. "What happens in two days?"

"I'm going to Connecticut to see Camilla Stafford and the house where the party is taking place. I'll need you."

"Margaret, I am required to return to my desk at United National next week, and I was planning to rest in preparation. The dollar is weak, they tell me. At least my stepfather reminded me of this a number of times while I was in Texas."

"Surely Carolyn Sue is not discommoded by the state of the dollar."

"I believe not, although she used this as an excuse not to increase my allowance. Not substantially, at least," he had the honesty to add. "In any case, Leila Parkins would be of more help than I."

"I don't believe Leila has a practical grasp of reality, however many debutante balls she's had." Leila Parkins's well-publicized career as a debutante had left her better prepared to attend parties than to give them.

"Nina Parlons, then."

"You wise darling! Nina knows all about party planning. But where is she? Not in New York at this time of year."

"Seattle," Paul said, "holidaying with her family. We keep up a correspondence, although she still does not consider me good enough for her. However, I feel that I may be altering her view of me as a worthless playboy."

De Vere signaled from across the room, almost impatient.

"I have to go now," Margaret said. "Nina. It will save me days of knowing who to call. Caterers and music and things. I'll ring her tomorrow."

Margaret and De Vere departed arm in arm into the hot, still summer night.

Chapter 6

"*Impressive sums* were invested to construct this house," Paul said. The Stafford estate glinted whitely in the morning sun. "But I wonder at its value in today's real estate market. The upkeep must be expensive."

"I imagine Matt Kessler could create very high-priced summer homes for the newly affluent if he had all this land to play with," Margaret said.

"No one appears to be at home," Paul said. The house did have a blank look, the cars were gone from the drive.

"Camilla will be here, she promised," Margaret said as they approached the front door. "Did I mention that we have unexpected assistance from Nancy's beau Richie? He has what Nancy calls 'connections,' although I don't wish to think what they might be. We have a promise that we will have no difficulty having the trash hauled away."

"You there!" A man's voice shouted, but the man himself was not visible. Margaret and Paul looked behind them down the drive, upward to the rows of gleaming windows and to the left toward the low garage. Finally a florid, paunchy man in green workpants and a grubby T-shirt emerged from a narrow gap in the high boxwood hedge at the edge of the drive.

"Nobody home," he said. "They don't like trespassers hereabouts. You better get back in that car and head for town."

"We are not trespassing," Margaret said grandly. "We are engaged in some business with Mrs. Stafford."

The man was still suspicious. "The Staffords are gone to

the city. I can't let you stay around. Orders."

"My dear Mr. . . . ?" Margaret was charming.

"Bert Thurman," he admitted reluctantly. "Head gardener. Jeez, nowadays the only gardener except for the boys who do the mowing. You got to leave."

"Mr. Thurman, Bert, you're exactly the person I need to see. I am Lady Margaret Priam, this is Prince Paul Castrocani."

Paul sighed quietly.

"Yeah? What you need to see me for?"

"Mrs. Stafford is planning a perfectly lovely party for Miss Camilla in September. Perhaps she's mentioned it?"

"Might have," Bert said evasively. "She doesn't do much talking to me, but that Rom person, the chauffeur, said something. Sounds like a lot of work for me."

"But you will only supervise, naturally," Margaret said. She thought of the twenty thousand dollars in the party account. A bribe would seem to be in order. "With an extra fee for your trouble."

"Well . . ."

"I will be arranging most of the details. Prince Paul is the liaison with our caterer."

"Ah, Margaret." Paul sounded defeated by the circumstances that had brought him to this.

"Now." Margaret became brisk and efficient. "I will look over the house and immediate surroundings. The maids can assist me. Prince Paul will go over the grounds with you to plan the location of the tents, the tables, the bars, the kitchens, the entertainment areas."

"Margaret, I don't believe I—"

Margaret faced Paul and smiled too brightly. "You're so knowledgeable about parties." Then, in a low voice, "And do be nice to Bert. Find out how long he's been at the Stafford estate. You know, whether he was here . . . back then."

Bert himself was clearly torn between agreeing to the demands of titled strangers and heeding the instructions of the lady of the house about trespassers.

"I guess if a maid shows you around, and I stay with the . . ." He looked doubtful. "Prince?"

"Definitely," Paul said. His faint accent had become quite pronounced.

"That's settled," Margaret said. "You two go about your business."

Paul and Bert strolled off. Paul had the authentic aristocrat's ability to get on amicably with the help.

The maid who answered Margaret's ring was the same young woman she had encountered on her first visit.

"You're Lady Margaret, right?" Her eyes flickered to the backs of Paul and Bert as they rounded the corner of the long garage. "You're to go down to the little beach. I don't know anything more than that." She opened the door wider. "I'll show you the way out through the front of the house."

Margaret followed her across the gleaming marble hall and through the solarium. Once again she tried to imagine where the battered body of Ann Stafford might have lain, how a young teenager might have entered and screamed, run to her mother, knelt beside her, and bloodied her hands to find signs of life. Or perhaps she had come into the house silently, heard terrible sounds in the solarium, had crept to the doorway, and hidden by the huge pots of greenery, had witnessed . . .

"Have you been with the Staffords long?" Margaret asked. "I don't believe I know your name."

"Dolores Wisniewski," the maid said. "This is only my second summer. I'm working to earn money for my tuition at UConn. The Staffords pay okay, but it's lousy work."

"A good deal of work is," Margaret said. "But why so here?"

"Very strict, Mrs. Stafford is. Camilla is about my kid sister's age. I feel sorry for her—they watch her like a criminal. I think it has something to do with her mother. You know about that?"

"Yes," Margaret said. "It was here, I think."

Dolores shuddered. "So they say. But there's nobody working here now that was around then, so it's just Cranford rumors. I remember when it happened. I was about eighteen, working up in Bridgeport, before I decided to go to college. My mother wouldn't let my kid sister out of her sight for months in case that crazy guy was still around." She stopped and turned to Margaret. "But you know what I think? The way they treat Camilla, it's almost as if they thought she did it."

"But that's impossible," Margaret said.

"That's what I think. She's just a scared kid, young for her age and trying to grow up sane in a kinda nutty family."

"You know them well, then."

"Hey, I'm just a maid for the summer," Dolores said. "I only know what I can figure out. Madame is too, too grand, Daniel is smooth but sort of bad-tempered. You've got to know your place around him. And that Nancy has a drawer full of pills. The brother breezes in now and then. They all treat Richie like he was a slug. Not that I blame them."

"Do you think," Margaret said, "just from what you've seen . . ." She leaned her head confidentially toward Dolores. Margaret, too, was awfully good with servants. "Do you think Camilla might have seen something that she's never told anyone?"

"From what I hear," Dolores said, "all she saw was the dead body of her mother."

"You won't say anything about me seeing Camilla," Margaret said.

"Not me," Dolores said. "Not on your life. Go out those doors and down the lawn."

"I know the way," Margaret said.

Dolores started back to the hall, then stopped. "They say around town that things were stolen when that murder happened. Some kind of silver dish, a little picture they say was real valuable, expensive junk these people have lying around. But look—they never learn. They got rid of some things, pictures and another big tapestry that used to be out in the hall, but there's still valuable stuff around for the taking."

"Are there no burglar alarms, or whatever?"

Dolores shrugged. "These old-time summer people think things are the way they used to be, that nobody would dare intrude on the high and mighty Staffords."

"But someone did," Margaret said. "Doesn't it make you nervous to be in the house alone after what happened?"

"No," Dolores said. "My brother in the Marines got me interested in judo. I could probably take out any little drugged thief before he knew what was happening." Dolores beamed confidently and went about her chores.

Margaret decided that it was the better part of wisdom to remove her high-heeled sandals before making her way across the lawn down to the beach. She wondered how that lawn would fare under the heels of a hundred dancing princesses at Camilla's party.

The tide was high, and only a small strip of fine sand showed between the gentle waves and the steep embankment where die-hard, stunted trees clung to the hillside. She was soon out of sight of the house and the grounds. A flat stone slab artfully placed for the purpose offered a seat. She had a view of the blue Sound with only a ruffle of waves. Very far out at sea, a tanker was making its slow way toward New York Harbor. Closer in, two sailboats tacked back and forth in the breeze.

Margaret went over her mental list of things Nina Parlons, in the course of a long phone call to Seattle, had reminded her must be done. Nina, who was successful at planning corporate parties for a select list of firms in New York, had given her names of the "good" caterers. Plenty of champagne, and never mind that the party guests would mostly be underage. Interesting food, at least two bands, imaginative decorations. Tents. Lighting. Party favors. Portable toilets, a powder room tent.

"Don't dream of letting them in the house," Nina had warned. "They'll burn it down."

Then the most important element of all: guests.

"What you need is numbers—it's like entering the lottery lots of times to be sure you win. Camilla has to be on other people's lists to be invited to the winter parties. Just be sure you invite the right social class, right heritage, right color, right religious persuasion. It takes a lot of effort to gather young virgins and eligible males and then keep them happy." Then Nina had added, "How is Paul?"

Margaret was happy to tell her. Not only was Nina a lovely and sensible young woman, she was quite rich. Overall, perfect for Paul, if he could persuade her that he was not a flighty half-Italian, half-American playboy.

Margaret looked up suddenly to see a tall girl with short brown hair and a steady look standing at the end of the beach. It had to be Donna Kessler. "Donna?"

"Yeah. Camilla will be here in a minute. She wanted to be sure you were alone." She started to leave.

"Wait, I've been wanting to talk to you."

Donna shrugged. "About the party? I can't wait. I wish I could be the debutante. . . ."

"It wasn't the party exactly," Margaret said.

The smile disappeared. "I don't know anything else we could talk about."

"About things . . . Camilla. About her mother—"

"It's not fair to talk behind Camilla's back," she said sternly. "She said you were a friend."

"I apologize," Margaret said, ashamed of herself.

Donna cheered up. "That's okay then. Come on, Cam," she called up the hill. Camilla scrambled down the embankment.

"You can go," Camilla said firmly. "I'll meet you at your house in a little while. If Grandmummy or Daddy shows up before I get there, tell them . . . tell them . . ."

"I'll tell them you were throwing up, and you went to my room to lie down, and you'll call them when you wake up. I'll make sure Dad doesn't give anything away." It seemed as good and practical a story as any Margaret could come up with.

"Okay. See you." Donna picked her way upward along some hidden path Margaret hadn't noticed.

"Well, here we are," Margaret said. "How did you get here from Donna's without being seen?"

"Through Cranford Hills, the new development. It's right next to our old bridle trails. We used to have horses when I was little. Daddy sold them. He said they were too expensive."

"Come sit down and tell me what you'd like for your party. I thought it might be nice to do it in the late afternoon. A sort of old-fashioned garden party. The girls could wear long dresses and big hats. There'd be candlelight as the sun went down. Fireworks when it got dark. Plenty of music of course," she added quickly. "And we'll find you a super dress."

Camilla seemed only vaguely interested.

"I know you don't like the idea of a debut," Margaret said finally, close to exasperation, "but, as I've said, your family wants it, and sometimes we have to do what our families wish."

Camilla gave her a long, too-wise look. "I've always done what they wanted. Well, I guess I was a problem about the dancing lessons and the patent leather shoes and the piano lessons. I hated all that. I tried because Grandmummy wanted me to, but Mummy didn't care. She stood up for me. Then she was gone." She sounded infinitely resigned. Margaret had to remind herself that Camilla was only nearing eighteen and acted much younger than most girls her age.

"Did you ever think that going through with this debut could mean a way to free yourself from your family?"

"Free . . ." Camilla looked out to sea. "Money makes you free. And then you can do good with it. Uncle Toby says . . ." Then she stopped.

"Even if you don't have the money yet, you could help with good works. Lots of debutantes do good works. There are so many charities that need volunteers." Margaret knew full well that the social charity game was not always what it pretended to be, and she was almost ashamed to be urging it on Camilla.

"My mother used to be on charity committees," Camilla said. "They sounded awful. I don't think she liked them much. Uncle Toby talks a lot about doing good, but the only thing I know he does is play piano with his group. He knows some neat people. But they're not invited here."

"I see," Margaret said. "Tell me more about your mother."

Camilla swung her head around and opened her mouth, but no word was heard.

"Not about the murder," Margaret said gently. "What was she like?"

"I don't know," she said slowly. "She and Daddy went out a lot when I was little, and they traveled. They . . . they used to fight sometimes. She didn't get along with Aunt Nancy, either." She shifted uneasily, perhaps guilty to be revealing family secrets. "Uncle Toby said she was ungrateful for all the good things she got out of our family. Aunt Lynne told me once she and my mother had been real poor when they were little, so marrying Daddy was her big chance. She always had pretty things. . . ." Camilla stopped. "I guess she liked men besides Daddy." She stood up. "I have to go back to Donna's."

"But we still have so much to plan. I'd like to look around the estate with you. Your grandmother mentioned the old playhouse."

"No, you don't want to go there. It's closed up and dirty."

Margaret shrugged. "Then let's find my friend Paul Castrocani who's walking around with Bert Thurman."

"No!" Camilla sounded frightened. "Bert might tell Grandmummy I was here. He's new here. He doesn't understand. And besides, I think Rom is around, and he's sure to tell."

"I see," Margaret said, and thought of the families that had worked for her family for generations, with little lying and no stealing and no telling of tales. "I'll go ahead with the arrangements, but you'll have to help with your dress. Something wonderful and romantic. I'm sure your grandmother will let you come to the city to shop."

"All right, if she lets me. It gets kind of boring here. Sometimes Aunt Nancy takes me to plays in New York. Aunt Lynne . . ." She rolled her eyes. "She wishes I liked to go shopping and have lunch. At least in the winter, I get to be in New York most of the time. Then I can go down to the Village to hear Uncle Toby's group. Sometimes."

"You're fond of your Uncle Toby, aren't you?"

"I guess so," she said. "I don't see him much. When I was little, he was around every summer, except when he was off with his friends. After my mother was killed—" She took a deep breath as she ventured into deeper waters where the story was not so well memorized. "He was the first one to come. When everyone else was here crying and shouting, with the police and everything, he was there to make them leave me alone."

"Are you ever afraid of being in the house because of what happened?"

"No," Camilla said. "That house doesn't frighten me. No one would want to hurt me."

Margaret was not so sure. Someone might, if someone thought she were saying things that had remained unsaid for several years.

A shower of small stones cascaded down the embankment, followed by Paul who was sliding—quite gracefully, Margaret thought—down the hill.

"This is Prince Paul Castrocani," Margaret said. "He has been known to make more elegant entrances. Paul, this is Camilla Stafford."

Paul dusted himself off and bowed to Camilla. "Delighted. I have been anticipating our meeting."

Camilla's careless slouch disappeared, she put out her hand with practiced grace, a proper little lady. "How nice to meet you. Thank you so much for helping with the party. You must find it terribly boring and silly." She looked very pretty all of a sudden, and she obviously liked the looks of Paul.

"I'm so sorry I have to be leaving," she said. "But I'm sure we'll meet again—certainly at my party."

"Certainly," Paul said.

As Camilla took the path up from the beach, Paul added under his breath, "I do enjoy adolescents' parties."

"Hush," Margaret said. "There will be a number of adults, although I don't think I'll be able to persuade De Vere to attend. Our principal problem will be obtaining a large group of young people and conveying them to this house."

"I presume you will require a trainful of them," Paul said as they followed Camilla's path. At the top of the hill, the Stafford lawn stretched up toward the house, while the path straggled into the woods at the lawn's edge. "At least there is plenty of space. Bert the gardener is doubtful about his ability to handle the grounds single-handedly, but I reassured him that your offer to hire others was genuine."

"Of course! You're a genius!"

"I do not believe it is too difficult to find help to mow the grasses," Paul said. "Merely a matter of money."

"No," Margaret said. "A train. An entire train, or at least several cars. Bring them from New York, send them home."

Bert was puttering with the sprinkler system for the nicely kept informal garden bursting with daisies and rampant begonias, bright blue lobelia and tall snapdragons. Away in the distance, almost hidden among feathery birches and low, dark pines was a small, white cottage, Victorian gingerbread with cupola and curlicues. Behind it rose deep woods.

"Everything seems to be in order, Bert," Margaret said. "You decide how many extra men you need."

"Thank you, ma'am. It will make things easier."

"Bert, I understand you were not here at the time of the murder," Margaret said.

"Murder?" Bert attempted to look blank. "Never heard of a murder hereabouts. 'Course I'm from upstate, near Waterbury." He wiped his hands on his hefty thighs. Nervous. "Oh, you mean the break-in some years back. Somebody got hurt."

"I was curious about the security arrangements now."

Bert frowned. "Nothing special. Locks on the doors, and that Rom fellow who drives for Mrs. Stafford. Wouldn't want to come up against him on a dark road. He's been with the old lady for years. I guess they think that's enough. Well, I got to work on the Eye-talian garden."

"Formal, enclosed. Quite nice," Paul murmured. "Some of the statuary might well be genuine. Very good copies, at least. You keep it beautifully, Bert."

"Thank you for that," Bert said, then he glanced over their heads toward the house and the garage wing. Margaret turned and followed his look. She caught a glimpse of someone who might be Rom, the family retainer, in one of the windows over the garage. He had been with the Staffords at the time of the murder, but he seemed more of a lurker in the shadows than someone willing to recall the past to a stranger like Margaret.

"We won't keep you from your work," she said. "Is that the playhouse down at the end of the garden?"

"Yep. Closed up, though, ever since I been here. I keep back the weeds and trim some."

"I see."

"I'll be turning on the watering system soon as you're out of range," he said and ambled off toward the back of the house.

"This has been a curious day. Camilla wanted me here, made a great effort, but for no reason I can think of."

"Perhaps she wanted to test whether she could trust you," Paul said. "I trust you did not mention her mother's death."

"We talked around it."

"Good," he said. "I don't like the idea of intruding on a family's private murder."

"Paul, dear. Murder is definitely not private. I will let it rest, for Camilla's sake, but I'd like to see that playhouse," Margaret said. "Come. Camilla definitely didn't want me near it."

"Not I," he said. "I will enjoy the view from the terrace."

As they separated and she headed for the playhouse, jets of fine spray rose from the ground and spun a mist over the garden.

The little house was well maintained; the front door was firmly locked. She peered through the slightly dusty windows and saw a drawing room, scaled down to a child's size. It was not a rough-and-tumble room but elegantly furnished with Victorian furniture painted white and upholstered in pastels. The only childish element, other than the size, was a row of pretty, old-fashioned dolls with bisque heads lined up on a shelf. Then she peered closer. On the polished wood floor was a pile of magazines, and a Coke can. Margaret tried the windows. They were unmovable.

She walked around to the back and looked in. Here was a child-size kitchen with cheerful chintz curtains and dishes in cabinets with glass doors. A small staircase rose to the upper story, and judging from the outside, there might be one or possibly two rooms on the second floor.

Margaret tried the door, and it swung open. "What luck," she said aloud and caught herself. The house seemed a place that was sometimes occupied. It was not simply the evidence of the empty soda can, but a sense that dust hadn't been allowed to settle as it does in long-empty rooms. She walked slowly into the little house, through the kitchen to the drawing room. The magazines on the floor were recent, teenage reading. Camilla must visit here, in spite of what was said to the contrary.

Standing in the middle of the drawing room, Margaret tried to imagine long-ago little Staffords playing quietly on a rainy summer's afternoon. She looked down. Curious. It seemed that there had once been a rug here, because the square of floor where she was standing was paler than the surrounding boards.

It took a moment to realize that there were sounds from above: a shuffle, the creak of a floorboard.

She froze. Someone was moving stealthily across the floor above.

Margaret moved toward the front door from the drawing room to the outside. It was as unopenable from the inside as from outside. In the distant garden, the jets of water twirled and hissed. Paul had long vanished to some sunny spot near the big house.

The only way out was the way she had come in—past the staircase to the floor where an unknown person walked.

Margaret, she thought, you've brazened your way out of

embarrassing situations before. No sounds from above now, and she breathed relief. Perhaps a large Connecticut mouse, or some woodsy creature that had found its way in.

Or a dangerous human who robs and murders . . .

She began to feel claustrophobic in the small room whose ceiling seemed to press down and whose walls were too close for ease. She edged toward the pretty little kitchen. Then she had a moment of real terror as heavy feet pounded down the stairs and the back door slammed.

The long silence encouraged her. Whoever had been there was gone.

Of course she had to look around upstairs. There were two rooms, a charming child's room with a lacy bed and gilt furniture. Another tiny room with a desk and bookcases filled with books. She looked through them: Winnie-the-Pooh, Beatrix Potter, illustrated fairy tales, and a couple of well-worn paperbacks—romance novels, Jacqueline Susann. Camilla's secret reading, or someone else's. Stuffed in between the books was a slim, leather pocket diary, now out of date by several years. She counted back. It was from the year that Ann Stafford had died. Curiosity impelled her to open it, and curiosity was rewarded. A folded sheet of creamy, heavy letter paper was stuck into the front. The engraved heading read:

STAFFORD
Cranford, Connecticut

Printed on the sheet in a dull pencil were the words: "You will be in danger."

Will be, she noted. Not *You are*.

Curious. She folded the note and put it in her handbag. A message to Ann Stafford? And from whom? Warning her of a danger that might arise if she failed to change something, ceased to do something, avoided a perilous course?

Was it a warning from a friend or an adversary?

Margaret eagerly leafed through the little book, with each week laid out across a double page. The first months of the year were filled with notations: hair appointments, a doctor's name, cocktails at seven with the so-and-sos, committee meetings, Camilla's name a few times with appointed hours, Toby's name, a few scattered *D*s—Daniel perhaps. In early summer, the name of Tannen & Oakes appeared a couple of times, with an early morning hour set aside. The summer rose to fullness, with dates for visitors to Cranford: Margaret recognized a number of well-known New York names. Tennis dates—Toby was a frequent opponent, Nancy only rarely. Then the pages were blank for the rest of the year. A life had ended. Margaret looked through the diary again. Not many clues, if any at all. She slipped it into her handbag.

In one of the desk drawers, she found a stack of the letter paper. A bottle of ink, but the ink had dried to a black powder. She took out the note she had found and looked again. The sheet was smudged, and one corner was curled. Ann had apparently saved it carefully for some time.

There was nothing more to see upstairs. Margaret went to look about downstairs, now that the house was empty of mysterious visitors. There was nothing to find here, either. Sunlight filtered through the trees outside and dappled the floor. In the kitchen, she found flowery handpainted china and dainty crystal glassware. But in a drawer, she found a leather box with a tray that held silver teaspoons, knives, and forks. Under the tray, she discovered another small box that held a collection of objects wrapped in tissue paper: a ring that might be a very large amethyst in a silver or platinum setting. A delicate miniature in a gold frame, the portrait of a lady from some centuries ago. A Mont Blanc fountain pen with a marbled finish, which Margaret thought was worth several hundred dollars. A broken chain made of fine silver links.

Margaret put the things back as she had found them, closed the box, and returned it to the drawer. Then she ventured through the spray to find Paul.

He was reclining on a lounge chair near a modest-size

swimming pool beside the guest house that had once been stables.

"It was far too hot in Texas to stay outside for a tan," he said. "I thought I would improve my appearance while the opportunity existed. You look a bit pale yourself."

She showed him the note.

"Margaret, this is the kind of trouble I am instructed to avoid."

"It's an old note. I think it was meant to warn Ann Stafford," Margaret said. "I found it in an old diary of hers. I think she spent time in the playhouse, when she wanted to avoid the family."

"But to me it signifies that there were matters going on that we do not wish to uncover."

"I won't involve you in my suspicions, if you don't wish it." She decided not to mention that there had been a person upstairs who might or might not have known that it was Lady Margaret below and not Camilla. "Let us stop for one moment at the house to speak to Dolores."

"Never knew anyone to be in that playhouse," Dolores said. "I think only Mrs. Stafford would have a key. Or that Rom person who's always sneaking around. If anyone takes care of it, it's not us maids."

"Quite charming," Margaret said. "Did anyone telephone while we were here?" She wasn't sure how loyal a servant Dolores was. In her own home, no Priam servant would dream of telling family business to a stranger, however amiable and titled.

"Mr. Toby Stafford telephoned some time ago. He asked if Miss Camilla was here. I said I hadn't seen her."

"Good. No point in causing her trouble. I saw the chauffeur a while ago. Would it be possible to speak with him?"

"Rom?" Dolores was disdainful. "What could you have to say to him? He's probably up in his apartment over the garage. I don't like the guy, so you've been warned."

"I see," Margaret said. "Thank you so much, Dolores. By the way, it won't matter much if you have to confess that Paul and I were here today. But you understand . . ."

"I haven't seen Miss Camilla," Dolores said.

"May I ask what it is you are studying at the university?"

"I'm thinking of becoming a lawyer," Dolores said. A telephone rang deep in the house. "Got to run. I'll catch hell if it's the family and it rings more than twice." She was gone.

Margaret did not have to face the chauffeur in his lair. He was standing at his post near the garage, not a big man, but he looked to be very fit. Indeed, no one would wish to meet him on a dark road.

"Mr. . . . um . . ." Margaret tried, but Rom was not helpful.

"The Staffords aren't happy about people tramping around the place," he said.

"We're preparing for the party in September," Margaret said. He merely stared at her through lowered lids. She tried again. "I understand you've been with the Staffords a number of years." He nodded. "I'm concerned about the security, since I have heard there was some violence a few years ago."

"You got nothing to worry about," he said. "That kind of thing doesn't happen twice."

"An intruder, I understand?"

"Yeah." He didn't sound convincing, and he did seem a bit nervous. "I wasn't here that day."

"Naturally not."

Rom glared at her. "I don't know what you mean by that, but she was okay, Mrs. Stafford was. It's not right for people to poke around in her business." Rom clearly meant Margaret.

"I'm not poking," she said. "I suppose you got to know her when you were driving her. Into the city, and the like. It's so difficult to drive oneself to appointments. Doctors and lawyers always seem to have offices on the most inconvenient streets."

"I work for the family," he said. "If one of the family

asks me to drive and Madame doesn't need the car, I do it."

His eyes shifted. Margaret was convinced that he did have a small secret or two about Ann Stafford's comings and goings.

"If you're expecting to wait around until Madame and Mr. Daniel return," he said, "they won't be back for a long time."

"We do have to be getting back to the city," Margaret said. "Thank you so much for your help." And let him wonder what kind of help he'd inadvertently given.

As she and Paul sped back toward New York City, mostly in silence, Margaret was moved to say, "I wonder whether Ann Stafford actually did have boyfriends. She was up to something."

Paul said, "If she was, nothing out of the ordinary."

"Not to the eyes of the likes of us, perhaps. It happens all too often in our so-called elevated social circles. But I believe the American public equates money with virtue, which makes transgressions all the more titillating. I wonder if you can find out with your vast banking connections how large a particular trust fund might be. Camilla's. I wonder who controls it."

"No. I will not become involved," Paul said.

"There's someone I'd like you to meet," Margaret said offhandedly as she flew over the Triborough Bridge and edged into the lane for the Manhattan exit. "Since Nina won't be back until the fall, I thought perhaps you'd like an introduction to a really marvelous girl whose father owns most of Sweden or Norway, or perhaps both. Tall, blond naturally, and totally carefree. She's in New York for a couple of weeks."

"How do you happen to have her conveniently waiting to bribe me?" Paul asked suspiciously.

"To tell the truth, Jytte was studying English history, God knows why, and she ended up at Priam's Priory because of some old Tudor who did something or other back then. She fell madly in love with my brother, who wasn't keen on her. He sent her across to visit the States. She has a suite at the Plaza-Athénée. Now, about that trust fund."

"I might make a very small effort to investigate."

"Good. By Tuesday, please. That's when I agreed to have dinner with Daniel."

Chapter 7

*M*argaret *thought* about the note she had found. Ann had been warned, and it hadn't saved her. Perhaps she believed that she would escape whatever dangers lay ahead. She looked again at the little pocket diary, but she could find nothing to suggest that there was anything significant contained in its pages.

Except for one thing. She took up her massive Manhattan telephone directory and looked up Tannen & Oakes. Whatever the firm was, it was located on Park Avenue.

Dianne Stark was at home for her call.

"Oh, sure. Very posh lawyers," Dianne said. "Robert Tannen is the man to see when you want a billion-dollar divorce. You should be talking to Lynne Jordan about him."

"He handled her divorce?"

Dianne laughed. "No. He represented her husband Philip, so poor Lynne had to make do with a more modest settlement than she expected. Are you planning to get married? A lot of people I know retain him before the ceremony, to be certain he'll be there afterward."

"No marriage on the horizon for me," Margaret said. "Someone mentioned the name. Let's get together soon, when my tasks as a party organizer are completed."

Margaret still had her five thousand dollars to earn, murder by friend or stranger notwithstanding. By Tuesday she felt that she had certain aspects of Camilla Stafford's party under control.

Joel Bergman, who had begun his career catering bar

mitzvahs in New Jersey and Italian weddings on Long Island, was now known as Josef LeBaron, caterer to the rich and celebrated. He had responded to every name Margaret managed to drop and had agreed to "talk over" the Stafford extravaganza.

"I do like Nina Parlons," he said. "If I can assist a friend of hers... And you know dear Leila, too!" He leafed through a thick volume bound in fine dark brown leather. LeBaron was carved deeply into the spine in gold. "I'm rather booked. September... right after Labor Day? Weekday, that's not too bad, but we'll be exhausted after the weekend."

"The Staffords want this to be really outstanding."

"I'm sure we can work something out." Josef LeBaron closed his book.

"Then you'll do it. For a price." Margaret was relieved.

Josef laughed. "The right price. I understand this isn't the formal coming out. More a wedge into the right circles."

"You are correct. She will make her debut this winter. This is simply a nice party, for... oh, say two hundred."

He shrugged. "As you wish. I will create the menu. They're saying that quiche is coming back, but it's simply not so. What would be fun? Something terribly British? A lovely trifle, of course. Perhaps a curry to remind one of the lost Empire? Pity it's the wrong season for a baron of beef. I'll work something out. The drinks—a fairly good champagne. The guests will be young, but they're quite, quite particular. However, they do understand the difference between a party by the sea and a ball at the Plaza. They'll make allowances. The underage question is the Staffords' problem." Josef LeBaron was in his element, making copious notes in his leather-bound book. "Do you have people to handle the rest? No? I can see to everything. Striped tents, I should think. Dance floor. Good flowers, perhaps hanging baskets with pastel streamers in the tents. And little nosegays of roses and baby's breath for the girls, don't you think? Lighting should be..." Josef puzzled that weighty problem. "Strings of fairy lights, tall candles on the tables. How does it sound so far?"

"Impressive," Margaret said.

"I subcontract everything but the food, but they're all excellent people. My waiters are really reliable boys and girls. No drugs, no drink. You'll have to see to the music, but I'll give you some names. At least two bands. Be sure you check on the wiring. Those rock groups use a lot of power. Invitations . . . not much time for printing, mailing, acceptances." Josef shook his head. "You may have to hand-deliver." He closed his book with a flourish. "Lady Margaret, I can promise you a party that will be simply to die for."

"Don't forget the balloons and the fireworks," Margaret said. "And the train."

"Train? Do you mean to transport them? Divine idea, but can one rent a train?"

"I don't see why not," Margaret said. "Aren't the railroads always in need of money?"

"You have a point there, but just in case, I think you ought to look into buses or helicopters."

She continued to be plagued by the Staffords. Calls from Eloise—yes, indeed, Eloise felt Camilla should shop with Margaret in New York for her dress; Eloise would check her engagements and see when she would be free to accompany them.

"I understand from Rom that you and an assistant visited Cranford," Eloise said. She sounded slightly irritated. "You must let me know the next time, so that Daniel or I can be on hand to advise you."

"It was Prince Paolo Sforza di Castrocani," Margaret said grandly. "Hardly an assistant."

Although Lynne had finally managed her escape to the earthly paradise of the Hamptons, she kept in touch. Rather, her secretary phoned to say that Mrs. Jordan planned to be in the city later in the week and definitely expected to lunch.

Daniel sent flowers, in anticipation of their coming dinner. An arrangement: birds-of-paradise and worse things with mauve leaves and bulbous blooms. Wispy fronds, a stalk of tiny green and beige orchids. It was perfect for a mausoleum, but not ideal for Margaret's apartment, which leaned toward chintz.

A postcard announced a performance by Toby's group in an obscure club very far downtown and very far off the beaten path. Nancy sent a completely illegible note.

Margaret felt as though she were being herded by a pack of determined sheepdogs.

"They're keeping watch over me," Margaret remarked to Paul when she rang him about the Stafford trusts. "I wonder if they know I've asked a few questions about the murder. Now, about the trusts..."

"I wonder that Camilla wasn't the victim," Paul said, "judging from the trusts. Large on paper, based on what Augustus Stafford left when he died. Eloise Stafford seems to have some personal wealth, and there is some for Daniel and his brother and sister, but most of the Stafford money appears to belong ultimately to Camilla, with the usual provisions for children unborn at the time of the writing."

"No siblings," Margaret said. "Not yet," she added.

"The grandmother is in control of the trusts; they are administered by Daniel Stafford. I cannot be certain of this, but I believe that the money can be used freely for Camilla's upkeep."

"Ah—a large summer house for her to live in, a townhouse for her to spend the winter in..."

"Paying for a very grand party or two," Paul said. "Correct. But I do not know much about these matters."

"But you are a banker!" Margaret said.

"Alas," Paul said, "I am not. That is a delusion harbored by others. It can be said that the Staffords have less than they once had, and that Daniel Stafford's management of the family's assets is not generally considered... brilliant."

"That would explain the sale of Stafford land to Matt Kessler," Margaret said. "I wonder if people looked into motives like money when Ann died. I wonder what would have happened if she and Daniel had divorced, and she left the family, except for her someday-wealthy daughter Camilla, whom she stood up for. I wouldn't dare ask De Vere more about the murder."

"Don't," Paul said. "He would blame me for not better controlling you. You have seen him?"

"We went to a film on Saturday afternoon. Although everyone claims to leave New York in the summer, there are many thousands who remain. And many of those attend films in air-conditioned theaters. I'm going to the Cranford house next week with LeBaron the caterer. Would you care to accompany us?"

"No," Paul said firmly. "All my free time is devoted to consoling Jytte for her rejection by your brother. I understand that her family owns both a fjord and a multinational conglomerate."

"You Italians are too easily taken in by blondes."

"True," Paul said. "Consider my father coming upon my mother in her vibrant youth—although I believe she has always achieved her blondness by some artifice. In any case, I cannot leave my desk here at the bank. If I work hard here," he said, "I may be given time off for good behavior."

Margaret returned the Stafford clippings to Poppy Dill.

"I'm rather in a rush to finish tomorrow's column," Poppy said. She was perched at her desk pecking at her old typewriter. "They want me to get a computer, but I'm too old and conservative. Was there a computer in the Oval Office when Ronnie was president? I prefer to think not. Now, what can I do for you?"

"I hope you'll include an item about Camilla Stafford's party."

Poppy sighed. "It's not really hot news. The Stafford name doesn't have much interest unless one brings up the murder, and that wouldn't be in good taste. Unless you have something to tell me?"

"Nothing at all," Margaret said. She longed to be able

to confide in Poppy, to tell her about the note, the unknown
person upstairs in the playhouse, her conviction that the
intruder story was all wrong, that Ann had not been killed
in the solarium at all. Margaret couldn't talk to De Vere
about it; he would be angry that she was involving herself.
Paul would refuse to listen. But Poppy would throw herself
into speculation with enthusiasm.

And then Poppy might feel a terrible urge to share the
speculations, if it meant putting her name on the front
page.

"Nothing," Margaret said, but in her mind she saw
Ann's body lying in a little room on a pretty, square pastel
rug that no longer existed. She imagined a man: angry,
jealous, frightened, overcome by some emotion. The servants were gone, the family was away, the daughter of the
house was in the village. If the body were carried to the
solarium, a few objects pocketed to suggest robbery . . .
Then escape for the murderer through the deep woods, and
no one to suspect that it was not a random violent crime.

Poppy took off her glasses and chewed on an earpiece.
"It would make some kind of an item if I could play up
your name as an intimate of the family."

"What?" Margaret shook off her imaginings.

"I mean you and Daniel as a current twosome."

"That might not please De Vere," Margaret said, without knowing precisely how De Vere would react to the
coupling of her name with an eligible figure in New York
society.

"Heavens, you could explain! Sam De Vere is a man of
the world, and a policeman to boot. They're used to all
manner of incorrect press reports."

"I did agree to have dinner with Daniel this evening."

"You see? The beginning of a story." Poppy beamed.
"In any case, for you I will put in a tiny item about the
party. There's not much happening until later in the fall.
But the more we can do to contrive a romance for you and
Daniel . . ."

"Oh, Poppy, no. Worse than De Vere, I'd have to face
the wrath of Lynne Jordan."

"Afraid you might go the way of Ann?" Poppy took a moment to type out another sentence of her column.

Margaret blinked. Could it have been an angry or jealous or frightened *woman* standing over the body?

"You know thcsc fronticr womcn, thrust into thc glamour of the big city," Poppy said gaily. "The lawless West and all that."

"I don't think Fresno is actually a frontier town, whatever else it might be," Margaret said.

"Lynne certainly didn't necessarily operate by the common rules of polite society," Poppy said. "She wasn't even kind about her own sister."

"Lynne spread gossip about Ann?"

"And carried tales to Ann, if it comes to that. Daniel has always been very attractive to women, and I don't doubt that Lynne made sure Ann knew all about any rumors that were flying. Perhaps she even implied there was something between her and Daniel—that would be purely fantasy, if you ask me." Poppy was eyeing her unfinished column. "Do be careful of Lynne."

Margaret was somehow not surprised to find Rom at the wheel of the Lincoln limousine when Daniel arrived to take her to dinner.

"Mother and Camilla came to the city for a few days," he said. "It can be so difficult to park, so I borrowed Rom."

Margaret thought that parking in midweek, midsummer New York could not be difficult—again, all it took was money—but did not argue. Daniel was playing rich and powerful, and she would go along with it. Rom appeared never to have seen her before in his life.

The restaurant was French, although not one of the Big Names. Margaret did not mention that she often dined at Chez Gaby and that darling Gabrielle, who owned the place and tended to everything personally, was quite an old friend. And a sensitive one. As Daniel made a show of being a knowledgeable admirer of fine dining, Gabrielle understood immediately that it was Daniel she was to greet as an old acquaintance, and Margaret was to be the stranger.

"Monsieur Daniel, what a pleasure. You are here just in time, since I am off to my little house in Normandy at the end of the week."

"Margaret, Gabrielle is a dear friend. This is Lady Margaret Priam, also a great friend."

"But of course she is," Gabrielle said. "I will send around a glass of excellent champagne we have only now received. Still quite rare in America. I will remind your waiter that we are especially honored tonight by our guests." A meaningful look told Margaret that Gabrielle would see to it that the waiter, who would also know her, would recognize only Daniel.

Daniel's intentions tonight were to beguile Margaret, impress her, charm her, win her heart.

How tiresome, she thought.

He cast about for common acquaintances. There were several. He talked about art. The recent show of Eric Fischl paintings he thought disturbing. The much-praised British musical opening on Broadway in the fall was not all that good—he'd seen it last fall in London. The stock market trembled, rose and fell, but did not trouble the Stafford fortunes. He spoke of countries and cities. He liked Geneva and Zurich, very neat and orderly; he didn't care for Spain but had enjoyed Rio. Did she like the Caribbean? He'd found a perfect little island . . . He pondered the menu, which Margaret knew quite well, and urged her to try his choices. He looked long and hard at the wine list. He was relentlessly charming.

Margaret was not immune to charm, but this was too much.

About the time the coffee and old brandy reached the table, she said, "Camilla said—"

"Said what?" Sharp. He had avoided any mention of Camilla during the entire meal.

"She said she still doesn't care at all about the party,"

Margaret said weakly. "It seems a terrible waste of time and money if she simply doesn't care."

"It is very, very important to the family," Daniel said. He looked down at his brandy glass, as though he could not meet her eye. "Mother feels—as do I—that this is the one way to restore our family to the position we are entitled to. People have whispered about Camilla since... since..."

"Surely no one thought that Camilla had anything to do with the murder. Why, that's as preposterous as saying Lynne Jordan did." She said it calculatedly, and she was not disappointed.

"I suppose you've heard from Lynne that my wife and I were not on the best of terms. There is far too much idle gossip around this city." He was momentarily cross. Then he said, "Margaret, you must understand that Ann and I were from two very diffcrcnt worlds, and she never did adapt to mine." The arrogance implicit seemed to escape him. "At the start, she got on with Mother, but the two of them couldn't agree on how Camilla should be raised. In the end, it seemed that Ann never understood me at all."

It was the first time in Margaret's experience that the wife who "didn't understand" had been dead for some four years.

"Oh, I do understand," Margaret said ever so sweetly. "She was from a different class. Unused to living with wealth and the finer things of life. The way you and I do." She was not proud of herself for uttering words she didn't believe. But all in a good cause.

"Exactly," Daniel said fervently. "I knew when we met that I could talk to you, and you'd know. ... Mother said she thought you had once been married but were no longer."

"True," Margaret said. Eloise also had been doing her homework, but Margaret was not prepared to explain anything about her past. "About Camilla," she began again.

"We have tried to be careful about the people she associates with," Daniel said. "She is known to be a wealthy young woman, even if she doesn't behave that way. We want to give her a fresh start and a happy future. We want her to forget all the tragedy she suffered. We suffered. I did love Ann once," he added. "She was a disappointment to me."

Margaret imagined that was so. She could remember loving her ex-husband once and being disappointed in him. But the Stafford marriage had lasted some fifteen years.

"You were married quite some time," Margaret said.

"We don't divorce as a rule in my family," Daniel said. "Except for Nancy. It might have come to that, but I thought that if we had more children, something to bring us back to the way we were." He might have said more, but the moment was shattered by the wholly contrived appearance of Lynne Jordan.

"Darlings! What a surprise! Pookie dear, look. It's Daniel and Lady Margaret. Let's just hover here a minute while Gabrielle sees to our table."

The oddly named Pookie was a very handsome, very young man, the kind who is so immersed in his own beauty that he looks blankly at the world around him, except when the world is attending to him. His role tonight was to make Daniel jealous.

"You've met Daniel, I think, my lovely brother-in-law. And this is dear Lady Margaret Priam. Pookie Mendocino."

"Ah, yes," Margaret said. "I knew Pookie's father, and you and I met when you were still a child."

Pookie's father had been a suave, ever-impecunious gambler and deal maker who had enjoyed London's private, high-stakes gaming clubs as he passed through England, even as he had passed through many a country with the constabulary at his heels. He had been to stay at Priam's Priory with Pookie in tow. Margaret remembered him as a precocious and ravishingly beautiful twelve-year-old who had responded to Margaret's remark that "Life could be difficult" with a serene "But not for me."

"Poor Daniel, you must be drained by this heat," Lynne said solicitously. "I know how hot weather bothers you."

"I thought you were in the Hamptons," he said. Margaret looked at him quickly. He spoke softly, but Lynne's intrusion on his evening with Margaret must have infuriated him.

"Eloise wanted me to come up to Connecticut for a few days," she said, "so I flew in this afternoon. She mentioned that you were in the city, but I had no idea I'd run into you."

"I understood Mother to say that she would be staying in the city until the weekend," Daniel said.

"Then I'll drive up with her," Lynne said, undaunted. "You'll be going up to Cranford for the weekend, of course."

"Yes," Daniel said. "Perhaps Margaret would like to join us. I'd like us to spend as much time with Camilla as possible."

"I think . . . I rather promised a friend . . ." Margaret began.

"Margaret will love our simple weekends at the shore," Lynne said, "unless she has a beau she doesn't want to leave behind. Come, Pookie. Our table is over there." Lynne stalked away.

"She seems to have an enduring attachment to the family," Margaret said when Lynne and Pookie were settled at their table.

"Yes," Daniel said. "She wants to remain part of the family."

Margaret glanced over at the couple and saw that Lynne was pretending she was not paying close attention to Daniel and herself. Margaret knew the look of a jealous woman. Lynne was regretting deeply that she had been party to inviting Margaret to work on Camilla's debut. The emotions Margaret had apparently aroused were making Lynn look rather old and pinched.

"And we all want what's best for Camilla," Daniel said. "What's best for the family. For our heritage."

And for the inheritance, Margaret thought, but didn't say it aloud.

* * *

Rom drove them through very mean streets to a very dingy and unsafe-looking building downtown, where, in a cloud of smoke—not all of it from leading filtered brands, they listened to Toby Stafford at the piano, a black bass player, and an Oriental drummer produce sounds rather too avant-garde for Margaret.

It had been Margaret's suggestion. It seemed the only safe response to a soulful look, a strong hand guiding her into the car, a manly knee pressed against her thigh. She did not want the next line to be "Your place or mine?"

Margaret blinked and squinted through the dimness to a shadowy shape beyond the raised platform where the musicians were. Surely that blond head couldn't be Camilla's. The girl was in profile, speaking earnestly to someone with his back to the room. Margaret squinted again. The profile showed a heavily made-up eye, a big hoop earring, a bright red mouth. Impossible. Toby's solo was a wild cascade of notes, and the rudimentary spotlight was turned on him. The bass player leaned his instrument against his stool and stepped down off the back of the platform for a moment. When Toby finished with a flourish and the rest of the trio joined in, the girl had vanished.

Toby carried a bottle of Molson's to their table between sets. With the lights up, it was clear that the girl was no longer in the room.

"What did you think?" Toby said.

Margaret was at a loss for words. Daniel was not.

"You'll never get rich," he said.

"I don't want to be rich," Toby said. Margaret noticed that he sported a Rolex watch worth several thousands.

"I found it interesting," Margaret said at last. "Camilla said she sometimes comes to hear you play. It's probably more accessible to someone who's accustomed to the style."

"I don't think Camilla's ever been here," Toby said blandly. "Mother would never let her hang out in this part of town. But I have played for her at home. She's appreciative."

"I'm trying to persuade Margaret to join us in Connecticut for the weekend," Daniel said. "I think I've succeeded."

Toby said, "I was thinking of coming myself. It's been years since I spent any time at the house."

Oh dear, Margaret thought. Can Nancy and Richie be far behind?

Chapter 8

Margaret had tried to resist the invitation. Daniel had insisted. Eloise had insisted. Lynne had made it clear that her own place was safely reserved at the house in Cranford. Nancy would be in residence, although not Richie, because of what was referred to as "business reasons." Toby said the club was slow on weekends.

If Margaret had surrendered, she had at least firmly held to her decision to drive herself up the Connecticut Turnpike to Cranford. She had decided that if nothing else, she would have one more try at prying information out of Matt Kessler.

De Vere had glowered when she told him that she couldn't see him because she had to spend some days in Connecticut. He had taken a couple of hours from being a policeman to sit with her in a garden cafe shut away from the steaming streets. He looked tired.

"I don't think these people are suitable companions. Miss Dill mentioned in her column that you have been seen with the Stafford man."

"Aha! You do read the society columns. I remember a time when you didn't know they existed. In any case, I was coerced into going," she said. "And as for Poppy's item, it was a trade. If she could mention me and Daniel in "Social Scene," I would be allowed a copy of a crucial list of available boys with the right addresses, restrained drinking habits, and correct manners when encountering elderly society ladies at formal functions. You shouldn't be concerned."

"But I am," De Vere said. "Did you know that the person who drives for Mrs. Stafford is a convicted felon?"

"Rom? How charitable of her to take him on. Did he do Ann's murder?"

"Apparently not. Mrs. Stafford swore firmly that he was driving her somewhere very far away. And Nancy Stafford —her current boyfriend is a violent character with reported ties to organized crime. Daniel Stafford himself is rumored to have been involved in doubtful financial transactions."

"You've actually looked into the family. What about Lynne Jordan? Toby Stafford?" She was trying to tease him, but she was touched that he was concerned for her.

"I know nothing about the Jordan woman. Toby Stafford had some run-ins with police when he was younger. Misdirected high spirits, I believe his lawyers said. These are not the right kind of people to consort with, even if they do have a well-known name."

"De Vere, I'll only be gone a few days, and you're busy."

"I know," he said. His jeans were pressed, his sports shirt was pristine, his loafers gleamed.

"Do coppers get jealous?" Margaret said.

"We can't afford to," De Vere said. "It's the jealous, angry, abandoned civilians who are allowed that luxury."

Now Margaret paced the very tasteful suite of rooms she had been given in the guest house at the Stafford estate and waited for the sun to come up on the second day of her forced visit to Cranford. At least she would soon be talking to Matt Kessler.

The sky was gradually turning a pale blue, heralding another hot late summer day. Bert Thurman had turned on the entire watering system to soak down the lawns and gardens before the sun was up, and the whisper of the sprinklers was the only sound.

"Shall I take a swim? Shall I eat a peach?" Margaret murmured to herself. The pool in front of the guest house, turquoise, clean, and still. And then there was the sea, down the hillside and hidden away from Stafford eyes.

The atmosphere in the house the night before, the first of her visit, had been tense. For some reason, Nancy had felt compelled to taunt her "darling brother" about his business acumen and to blame him because her funds were low. Margaret thought she might have partaken of substances that loosened her tongue. Lynne had hovered about Daniel so closely that he had sharply asked her to leave him alone. She had spent the rest of the evening glaring at everyone and especially at Margaret.

No one had seemed especially pleased to find Toby true to his word. "Dan said we were having a family gathering. I'll bunk down in my old room on the top floor."

Then he had slapped Daniel on the back and asked him if he'd met any nice girls lately. "You got to watch this guy," Toby said.

"*Have* to," Eloise murmured automatically.

"Even dear Mother agrees," Toby said cheerfully. "Where's Camilla?"

"I sent her to bed," Eloise said. "She started talking about her mother."

"God, Mother. She's nearly an adult. You don't send kids that age to bed because they say something that sparks some kind of guilt in you." Toby shook his head.

"She wasn't talking about Ann," Nancy said, beginning to slur a little. "She was talking about mothers. She was talking about children who don't have mothers. Little black children in the ghetto."

"We don't speak of such things," Eloise said. "And I have no guilt." Suddenly she remembered that Margaret was sitting quietly, the stranger in their midst. "Margaret, you must think us dreadful to carry on. There's something about Toby that creates dissension in our ranks."

"I take it as a compliment that you feel so at home with me," Margaret said. She had felt a bit uncomfortable when Camilla's innocuous comment had annoyed Eloise enough to dismiss her from the evening.

The one curious note was a whispered remark from Camilla: "Mr. Kessler wants to speak to you privately. Here's the telephone number." She handed Margaret a tiny slip of paper. Shortly thereafter, Camilla had been sent away, with no opportunity for Margaret to pry from her a truthful statement about whether she had been at Toby's jazz spot.

Margaret had excused herself to fetch a wrap from the guest house and telephoned Matt. He would meet her at the little beach in front of the Stafford place very early the next morning.

"I've been thinking," he said. "We ought to talk. I'll come around to the beach by boat. I keep a little Boston Whaler at the town dock."

The sun was just up now, turning both the sky and the ocean blue. Margaret slipped on a beach robe over her swimsuit and walked along the edge of the lawn, down to the cove, thinking all the time that eyes were watching from behind still-drawn curtains.

This time, she found Camilla's secret path and found herself in shadow on the little beach. It was still quite cool out of the sunlight, and Margaret touched a tentative toe to the water. Cold. She listened for the sound of a boat engine but heard only the gentle hiss of the waves lapping against the beach.

It was still too early for Matt, so she bravely waded in, gasping as the cold water hit her stomach. The sandy bottom sloped quickly, and soon she could no longer touch it even with her toes. She swam out beyond the curve of the land and looked east, from where she imagined a boat would appear. The sun was glinting fiercely off the waves, and the sea was empty.

Margaret treaded water and waited, but the only boats that appeared were a sleek power boat that headed straight out into the Sound and quickly became a dot on the horizon, and a small sailboat putting out from the distant shore. She swam back to the beach.

Her watch resting on her robe told her that it was past the appointed hour for Matt. A change in plans? Waylaid by an eager potential property buyer? A household crisis?

Perhaps his new wife didn't like the idea of him meeting a strange woman on a beach before the sun was well up.

Since Margaret was a conscientious woman, especially when she had been paid five thousand dollars to do a job, she carried in her head orderly lists of things to be done, things that had been done, things that would never get done for Camilla's party. As she waited for Matt, she leaned against a fairly comfortable rock she had covered with her robe and thought with her eyes closed about the virtues of chiffon gowns and the imminent return of quiche to the fashionable menus of America.

The noise startled her: a crash in the brush above the beach on the side of the embankment that had not been cut back and tended. She sat up and shaded her eyes toward the hill and saw to her dismay that a huge log—almost an entire tree—was bouncing and tumbling down the hillside, along with a scattering of fairly large rocks. It took a crazy path, soared off a boulder, and came flying down to the beach.

It landed quite close to the spot where Margaret had been meditating on the ins and outs of debuts, but Margaret had removed herself to the most distant part of the little beach.

"You will be in danger," she said aloud. She shaded her eyes and looked up the hillside, hoping to see Matt Kessler scrambling down full of apologies for having taken the land route and dislodging a fallen tree. Or perhaps Lynne had decided to take a more active role in warning her off Daniel.

It took some effort to remove her robe now lodged under the heavy log.

Matt Kessler never appeared.

"Did you have a morning swim?" Eloise asked. There was a large buffet breakfast in the long dining room, but only Eloise was there.

"Yes, lovely," Margaret said. She had decided that large pieces of wood don't move of their own accord, except during earthquakes, and that had not been the case this morning.

"We had some sad news this morning," Eloise said. "Our friend Matt Kessler."

In spite of herself, Margaret's voice was not steady as she asked, "That nice man I met? What happened?"

"An auto accident," Eloise said. "We don't know the details. He apparently ran off the road on his way to the bay where the townspeople keep their boats. I've always said that road was dangerous. Rom dislikes it. Very narrow with a lot of curves. Matt may have been driving too fast and met a car coming the other way."

"Is he . . . dead?"

"Not as far as we know. Poor Donna called Camilla too early this morning. My dear, that doesn't seem like enough food to keep you going until lunch."

"I never eat much in the morning," Margaret lied. She did not wish to say that threatening coincidences always robbed her of her appetite.

"Then there was another car," Margaret said.

"We only presume so. Matt may just have been terribly careless. We're going to the country club for lunch. There are still some nice families who belong. Do you play golf?"

"Not really," Margaret said. "Tennis some."

"You and Camilla should use our courts this afternoon. Perhaps doubles with Lynne and Daniel. Nancy claims to like to play, but she's quite bad. In any case, she's already gone off to meet that person. . . ." Richie was to remain nameless. "He's taking her off somewhere for the day."

"About Mr. Kessler."

"I'm sure we'll hear any news. Ah, Toby, we seldom see you up this early."

Toby looked like a sleepy bear in a fuzzy terry cloth shirt and baggy sweatpants.

"Been up and about for hours, Mother. I get to the country so seldom I have to take advantage of it. A swim in the pool, a run along the old bridle path. Sound body, fairly sound mind. What is this I hear about old Matt?" He sounded especially cheerful.

"An accident," Eloise said shortly. "Where is Daniel?"

"The very words spoken a moment ago on the terrace by the lovely Lynne. I imagine he's still abed."

"No," Eloise said, "he's not. I heard him leaving the house quite early. He should be here to entertain his guest."

Toby turned to Margaret and looked her in the eye. "What did I tell you? Bliss."

Margaret was less interested in Toby's teasing than in wondering whether someone might have overheard Camilla's message or listened in on her telephone call to Matt. If it was so important to frighten her and silence Matt, she would prefer to be among friends, safe at home in New York City.

Camilla came hesitantly into the dining room. Margaret thought she looked tired, too tired for a healthy teenage girl. Although she wore a bright pink T-shirt with her cutoff jeans, even the lively color wasn't adding many roses to her cheeks.

"I'm sorry about your friend's father," Margaret said.

"I talked to Donna again," she said. "They said he won't die or anything. He's unconscious, and his leg is broken and some other things."

"Luncheon at the country club at one," Eloise said briskly. "Camilla, I want you to wear that pretty little dress with the embroidery that I had made for you in France by that clever woman."

"Yes, Grandmummy."

"Since we have hours before lunch," Margaret said brightly, "why don't we take a lovely walk? Into the woods, down the road, off to the beach . . ."

"I have some business to attend to this morning," Eloise said. "Perhaps later."

"Camilla and I," Margaret said and was firm. "A nice healthy walk."

"Well . . ." Eloise frowned.

"We'll go as soon as Camilla's had breakfast," Margaret

said. "I need the exercise." Centuries of Priams won out handily over a mere century of Staffords.

"I never eat breakfast," Camilla said.

Eloise sighed, defeated.

Toby spoke up then: "Leave them alone, Mother. Must you always have both the last and the next-to-last word, and haunt the child even on an innocent walk?"

"Kindly define innocent," Eloise said. But she turned away and quite nearly tossed her head proudly as she departed the room.

Camilla and Margaret went out into the sunshine.

"Would there be a quick way to the village?" Margaret asked. She was hoping she would have a chance to work around to having seen Camilla at Toby's club, and all her other questions, without the whole family popping up at any odd moment. "There is something I need to buy."

"The maids would see that someone got you anything."

"I'd rather I did it myself." Margaret was thinking of a safe public telephone box in the middle of Cranford, with no curious listeners.

They started off past the gardens, which were more extensive than Margaret realized, past high hedges behind which rose slim, dark cypresses, and then into the carefully tended woodland. Bert Thurman ranged far and wide about the estate. Camilla brought them to a broad, cleared trail fenced on either side and lined with trees whose branches overhung the trail.

"This would be the old bridle trail," Margaret said, "but it appears that vehicles sometimes pass this way." There were tire tracks in the soft earth.

"It's kind of a back way," Camilla said. "The Cranford Hills development is over there, and there's a way into our property. The short cut to the road to town is up ahead."

"I see. I didn't notice your father about this morning."

"Daddy might have gone for a sail with somebody at the yacht club. Or maybe he's playing golf."

"I looked in at the playhouse the day Paul and I were here," Margaret said casually. "I imagine you go there to get away from the family, the way your mother used to."

Camilla stopped and looked at Margaret warily. "It's closed up. I don't go there."

"Surely you do," Margaret said. "I won't tell anyone."

"How did you know?"

"Magazines on the floor, empty Coke can."

"I do, sometimes," Camilla said slowly. "It's a private place away from the others. You can't even see it from the house. I found the key among Mummy's things, after . . . A couple of years ago. But no one else can get in."

"I see," Margaret said and thought that heavy-footed visitor she had just missed seeing had certainly found a way in.

"Did anyone know your mother used the playhouse as her retreat?" Someone, for example, who might leave a note that truthfully stated, "You will be in danger."

"I don't know," Camilla said. "I knew. Maybe Aunt Lynne did, too, because she . . . she likes to know things. But I never went there until after Mummy died."

Had Camilla looked through her mother's diary? Margaret wondered. Did she ever see that note? Did she hide the box of treasures in the drawer in the kitchen?

"Did you ever see—?" Margaret began.

"I didn't see anything," Camilla said, sounding a little desperate, and Margaret was ashamed of herself for pressing.

Sunlight dappled the broad pathway they walked, and Margaret conjured up old memories of exhilarating canters of her youth, alone on a good strong horse in the early morning. How untroubled her youth had been compared to Camilla's.

Margaret still wanted to ask about seeing Camilla at Toby's club on Tuesday, but now it seemed too cruel.

Suddenly Camilla stopped ahead of Margaret and stood with her back to her. "I saw you at Toby's club," she said unexpectedly. "Why are you spying on me? Did they ask you to? What did Daddy say?"

"I'm not spying," Margaret said. "It was purely chance that we were there. I don't think your father saw you, and I didn't tell him. That is the truth. Except that I've been very puzzled about the stories of your mother's death. I keep wondering if you know something you've never told anyone."

Camilla looked around at Margaret. "I'm afraid to know. I don't think about it. You've got to understand."

"I do," Margaret said. "But you might be in a dangerous position."

Camilla tossed her head. "Nobody wants to do anything to me. And I can take care of myself."

Margaret admired her assurance. "I suppose Matt Kessler thought he could take care of himself, too."

"It was an accident," Camilla said, but she didn't sound quite so assured. "This way," she said suddenly. "Be careful of poison ivy." She stepped off the bridle path and climbed over a low stone wall. A narrower path with a wild tangle of brush on either side led downhill a short distance. Then they were on the main road, past the turn onto Stafford Road and quite close to the village center and the desired telephone.

Margaret chose the drugstore. While Camilla examined the cosmetic cases without much interest, Margaret found a pay phone and dialed New York.

Paul was at home and not quite awake.

"Do this for me, please," Margaret said. "At about eleven, ring me at the Stafford house. Be anyone—not yourself—who has an urgent need to see me in New York this afternoon. Maintain the fiction. Someone might be listening."

"This sounds serious," Paul said.

"Not terribly. Some threatening gestures, possibly perpetrated by one of the Staffords, although I can't determine which."

"Perhaps you are being too suspicious."

"I think not. Matt Kessler was run off the road this morning as he was on his way to have a private talk with me. Then someone rolled a rather large piece of forest down the hill to the spot where I was sitting on the beach, awaiting Matt. And finally, I'm convinced that Camilla believes that someone in her family had something to do with her mother's murder, but, poor child, if she says anything, she'll destroy whatever family she has left."

"Then it is serious!" Paul sounded alarmed. "You must leave at once."

"Your call will make it possible to retreat graciously and without alerting the family to my suspicions."

"I believe you should give up your endeavors on behalf of Miss Stafford," Paul said. "I am sure that De Vere would agree."

"Please don't mention this to him," Margaret said quickly. "And I can't stop now. I have to help Camilla make a start getting away from them."

I sound like Toby, she thought, then added, "I don't care to give up my fee, in any case. I have plans for it."

Chapter 9

"*And this* is the end of your detecting," De Vere said. He—and not Paul as she had expected—had been waiting for her at the apartment he and Paul shared. Paul had contrived to vanish for the day, after he had phoned the Stafford house to announce grandly that Giovanni Pergolesi must speak to Lady Margaret Priam immediately. His accent was perhaps overdone, as he explained to dear Lady Margaret that if she were not in New York to sign certain documents before the banks in Geneva opened for business in the morning, he would not be responsible.

"I shall return to the city immediately," Margaret had said. "I hope my hostess will understand."

"But naturally she will understand," Paul said. "It is the way of the world we live in."

Eloise was not pleased, but naturally she understood.

Now, expecting to see Paul, Margaret was facing De Vere, who definitely did not understand.

"Paul shouldn't have told you," Margaret said.

"Like me, Paul is concerned about your welfare." He faced her and put his hands on her shoulders. "I don't do well expressing my feelings," he said. "I'm not sure how I feel sometimes, especially when you get spoiled and stubborn." He put his arms around her and held her close for a moment. "I do care too much to see you harmed." He released her and walked toward the windows that overlooked the first floor tenant's tiny but artfully arranged garden.

"De Vere, I can't stop the party plans, but I promise to

be careful." If she told him of Camilla's suspicions, she had no doubt that he would have her locked up to prevent her from continuing.

De Vere sighed. "These people are not going to leave you alone. You're poking into their private business. You of all people should know how that class feels about privacy, especially if they're hiding a crime."

"Then you do think one of them murdered Ann Stafford!"

"I don't think anything of that sort," he said crossly.

"It's my duty to stand by Camilla. I promised her."

"Your reasoning is exceptionally weak," De Vere said.

"The least I can do is find her a decent dress for this party," Margaret said. "It's quite impossible to get Mrs. Stafford and Camilla to agree on anything—color, fabric, style, the choice is yours." But De Vere was not interested in questions of fashion. He looked at her sternly.

She said, "I do promise I won't poke around anymore. I won't let myself be trapped in their house with them. I'll simply do my job."

"And I, I'm afraid, must do mine. I have to see some men about a violent crime. The money involved is new and clean, laundered in fact. Will you be free tomorrow evening?"

"More to the point, will you be free? I am."

"Good," he said.

"Now I think I ought to find myself a consultant. A genuine debutante."

Leila Parkins, who had once been a celebrated debutante and who was now an even more celebrated society personality, was passing through New York from Europe to the West Coast. Margaret had read the details in Poppy's "Social Scene" column and had decided to impose on their acquaintance. She suspected that Leila did not think much about matters that didn't relate directly to her, but she certainly retained memories of the days when she was heralded as the Deb for All Seasons.

Leila had chosen a fashionable restaurant that provided a crowded sidewalk cafe where the tables spilled out to block the progress of envious citizens, but which was so fabulously exclusive that habitués didn't mind sitting in the midst of heavy traffic pollution—not to mention within eye contact of ordinary New Yorkers.

"You look divine," she purred at Margaret. Leila had managed to get one of the most select of the select tables, a spot where she could readily be photographed should a wandering paparazzo happen by with his camera.

"And you look healthy," Margaret said.

"Costa Smeralda," Leila said. "I missed Kay by only a few days."

Margaret understood that the Aga Khan alighted at his resort on Sardinia from time to time, but she did not believe that he would regret having missed Leila Parkins, if indeed he knew her at all.

"Being a debutante? I hardly want to dredge up those deb days." Leila shuddered elegantly. "Nothing but parties and teas and luncheons and those boys! But I had a really fabulous dress for my ball. Strapless, although I don't know how I got that trick past Mummsie. And she loaned me her pearls. A simple double string, but with this marvelous clasp, lots of diamonds. But Margaret, darling. Camilla Stafford? You can't turn hopeless material into a debutante. You have to start practically at the absolute cradle. Little white gloves, dancing lessons, how to talk to servants, how to drink champagne. How to dress, how to walk. How to be nice to dreadful old ladies who knew your great-aunt Felicity way back before time began. It has to be in your blood, if you want to have a good time as a deb." Leila was in her early twenties, but she made it sound as though it all happened eons ago instead of three or four years before. Margaret thought she had probably already invested money from her enormous trust fund in Retin-A stock, so as to be totally prepared for the onset of wrinkles.

"I promised to do what I could for Camilla," Margaret said.

Leila waved to someone across the avenue. "Those

Staffords have an awful reputation for slaughtering unacceptable family members, don't they? The wife of that divine Daniel Stafford. I think it happened the year I came out actually, so I heard the talk. Mummsie and that man she's married to now don't think much of the Staffords. Of course, they're known to be careless with their capital." Leila made it sound like all the Seven Deadly Sins rolled into one. "Camilla is supposed to be odd. You see her sometimes at the downtown clubs, but never with people one knows."

"I don't doubt that," Margaret said, "but she's very sweet and innocent." Camilla at Toby's jazz club hadn't looked shy and demure. She imagined that Toby enjoyed abetting Camilla's secret life.

"Ha! So you say. I doubt that." Leila shrugged. "I suppose you need names to invite, really good ones. Then people will invite her, and so on. If she behaves herself. That woman she's related to—no, not Nancy. People understand about Nancy. I mean Lynne Jordan. Such a nouveau, no taste, no class, but you see her simply everywhere. People like that are bad for a girl's reputation."

Leila, whom Paul Castrocani had once deemed the ultimate catch of the day, tossed her blond curls and stood up. "I have a limo on hold somewhere around the corner," she said. "It's to get me to the airport on time, although they're divine about holding the plane for me. Let's have lunch in the fall." She leaned over and brushed cheeks with Margaret. Then she said, "Remember, she'll need a nice little dress, and do see that she has a tan. It looks so good with white."

"The dress is a minor problem," Margaret said. "The grandmother insists on helping to select, Camilla resists. . . ."

"But it's so simple!" Leila said. "I have tons of adorable little garden party dresses I'll never wear again in a million years. Why don't you borrow one or two? Go around to my place at the Olympic Tower." Leila inspected her adorable dimples in a compact and slipped on her dark glasses.

"I should move, but I've been hanging on for sentimental reasons. Morley Manton decorated the place for me for almost no money. My cleaning lady is there today. She'll let you in, and you pick out something, have it altered, whatever. I mean, don't get into the Valentinos, and don't touch my old Christian Lacroix pouf, that's already a museum piece, but see if there's something. It will save you a lot of trouble. Give my love to Paul, if you run into him. *Ciao*."

How refreshing she is, Margaret thought. Barely a brain in her head, but what there is knows what's important.

"I can't have you stealing Miss Leila's dresses." The cleaning lady was indignant.

"I have this little note from Miss Parkins," Margaret said. "I'm only borrowing one or two."

Marva looked Margaret over, and decided she was authentic and obviously not a criminal. She read Leila's note.

"Sounds all right," she said, "but when you leave, you'll show me what you have in that big pocketbook and in your pockets. No offense, but Miss Leila has a lot of pretty little things around, nothin' too valuable, but nice. I ain't going to have you make off with anything, or I could lose my job. Won't mean anything to you if you take away some little silver picture frame or a bit of gold jewelry, but I got to answer. . ."

Margaret had ceased to listen and was gazing across the room at the white linen wall and the big, puffy mauve linen sofa and the huge, round glass table on which rested just such a pretty little silver picture frame with a photo of a young and laughing Leila between what appeared to be a mummy and a daddy.

"One can't be too careful," Margaret said finally. "Little treasures, memories of childhood, little family heirlooms."

"You got it," Marva said. "Miss Leila's bedroom and dressing room are down the hall. The closet takes up half the space. Just don't leave without seeing me."

Margaret, who had herself seen pretty much everything

in her world, was not entirely prepared for the array of finery that Leila's closet held.

For her own amusement, she held up the Lacroix and seriously doubted that satin cabbage roses, flounces, poufs, and *bustiers* would survive the test of time. The Valentinos were elegant. There were some trendy but attractive Herreras and Roehms, a slinky Halston from his glory days, and a red Scaasi that Margaret recalled seeing Leila wear at some affair.

At the end of the long closet were hanger upon hanger of more girlish gowns in pastels and whites, each in its own plastic cover. Camilla was slimmer, less busty, a bit shorter than Leila, but Margaret picked out half a dozen delightful dresses that might do with some alteration.

She eliminated dresses until she had three, then two, and then chose. Pale yellow—Camilla looked well in yellow. A satin underdress was covered with flowing pale silk chiffon embroidered (that would please Eloise) with tiny flowers in darker shades of yellow, with just a few scattered brilliants to catch the light. Camilla would sparkle within the bounds of good taste. It had full, flowing sleeves, gathered at the wrist, and a square neck that wasn't daringly revealing (Eloise would also like that). Margaret imagined Camilla in her long flowing gown, hair pinned up, with a few ringlets framing her face, the right amount of makeup to accent her eyes. She wondered if Eloise had pearls to loan. Of course she had pearls.

"No, we'll save the pearls for this winter," Margaret said aloud.

"You speaking to me?" Marva stood at the door, duster in hand. "Lord, don't I wish I had the figure to get into one of those bitty dresses." Marva was ample in all of her body parts.

"Even as do I wish," Margaret murmured. "What do you think?" She held up the yellow dress.

"There's nobody can let that out enough for you, honey," Marva said. "No way."

"It's not for me. It's for a young girl who's had some

sadness in her life, but she's having a party all for herself. I want her to look really special."

"That one will do it," Marva said. "I'll fetch you a box to take it away so it won't get mussed. But," she added sternly, "I'll see to the closing and taping if you don't mind."

Impulsively Margaret took a second dress for Donna, slightly less spectacular as was appropriate for a best friend. Leila would probably never notice.

"I will be good from now on," Margaret said aloud as she departed the Olympic Tower with a neatly prepared dress box in hand. She said it in the direction of Saint Patrick's Cathedral, gray and spiky and gothic across the street from the Tower's entrance.

Margaret looked in at Kasparian's shop from time to time, to be certain the burglar alarms were functioning (even though every precious oriental antique was locked up behind walls of steel). On one such midmorning visit, she found her friend Dianne Stark strolling past on Madison Avenue.

"Charlie"—this was Dianne's rich, older, doting husband—"insists on going to work like other people, so we're in the city a good deal," she said. They went to lunch at a place where nobody they knew would dream of going. What they spoke of had nothing to do with Staffords, until they indulged in sinful desserts.

"My little party is under control," Margaret told Dianne. "Josef LeBaron is quite divine about handling everything. Acceptances are gratifying. Really good people." Margaret giggled. "I'm beginning to sound like Eloise Stafford."

"I've always found the Staffords to be disagreeable people. Full of themselves. Charlie and I run into them at these charity things we can't get out of. Most Old Money are fairly decently behaved, and polite even to me who came from out of the blue, as it were." Dianne enjoyed the fact that she who once served the public on cross-country flights now was served by others. "The same can't be said of the Staffords, although Daniel once tested the romantic waters in my vicinity."

"How did he do?" Margaret asked.

Dianne laughed. "Sank. Charlie is noncommittal about Daniel, but I know he doesn't care for him. They belong to the same clubs, manage the same kinds of money things. I believe Eloise was severely snubbed in the distant past by Charlie's mother when she was a social power, so she snubs me in return. She probably remembers that, like me, her ancestors only go back to the day before yesterday."

"Oh dear." Margaret spotted a familiar face across the restaurant. "How on earth did Lynne Jordan ever think of this place? Has she seen us?"

"I'm afraid so," Dianne said. "Another disagreeable person. I warn you, I shall have a pressing engagement if she joins us."

Lynne joined them with shrill chirps of feigned surprise. Dianne took herself away immediately on her pressing engagement. "I warned you," she whispered to Margaret as she left. "Do call if there's anything I can do." She fled from Lynne, who seemed willing to endure this uncongenial luncheon spot for as long as Margaret chose to endure her.

"So glad she left," Lynne said. "Such a common person. From nowhere, but just look at her. We have to talk. There's trouble."

"Really?" Margaret could think of nothing that was not moving smoothly with her part of the party and could only think that something had happened to Camilla.

"Camilla. She's becoming impossible. She's talking about refusing to go on with the debut plans."

"How odd," Margaret said. "I spoke to her yesterday afternoon, and she sounded enthusiastic for a change."

Lynne's eyes flickered, and Margaret saw that she had been lying.

"In truth, it's Daniel who's beginning to have second thoughts."

"Could it be that you're having second thoughts?" Margaret asked. "Daniel seems to be perfectly happy. With me," she couldn't help adding. Really, Lynne Jordan was too much.

Lynne leaned across the table. An unseemly row of beads of perspiration was forming on her brow. "Are you sleeping with him?" She looked dangerously intense.

Margaret summoned a cool, disdainful stare. "Naturally not. Bad form to sleep with the man who's paying you."

"How dare you!" Lynne leapt to her feet and her chair toppled over. In this quiet neighborhood lunch-brunch-drinks-at-day's-end sort of place, no hovering waiter rushed to right the wrongs done to respected patrons. Lynne left the chair overturned.

"Stop it at once," Margaret said. "I have no interest in Daniel Stafford."

"Why I ever asked you to help me with Camilla..."

"You gave good reasons," Margaret said.

"Don't expect me to do you any social favors," Lynne said.

Margaret, secure in the knowledge that she had never had to ask anyone for anything that involved society, said, "I will not ask for any." Before Lynne could flounce away dramatically, Margaret signed a credit card slip with a flourish and stood up. "I have quite a number of matters to attend to," she said. "The party is only a week away."

Chapter 10

*W*hen *the* day arrived, the weather was satisfyingly fine. Josef claimed it was the LeBaron magic at work. At least one thing was going to be all right.

Margaret went upstairs to the room where Camilla was dressing. It was one of the impersonal guest rooms with a three-way mirror so that Camilla could view Leila's borrowed gown from all angles. It had been altered by Dolores Wisniewski's aunt in the village to fit perfectly.

"You look terrific," Margaret said. "Are you excited?"

Camilla shrugged. Dolores, who had volunteered her services, was putting the last touches to Camilla's hair. Donna Kessler was at the windows that looked out on the lawn where waiters were scurrying and the fireworks man was checking the placement of the roman candles, shooting stars, and fiery fountains on the embankment over the water. Donna looked quite alluring in demure dotted swiss that trailed romantically behind her.

"This is going to be great," Donna said.

"Will your father be able to come tonight?" Margaret asked. She hadn't been able to speak with Matt since the accident. He was, quite pointedly, not available to her.

"I don't think he's coming."

"Grandmummy called him this afternoon," Camilla said. "She told him not to come." She had an odd sort of smile. "What she said was that he needn't trouble himself, we'd look after Donna. But I knew she meant he wasn't to come."

"That's it," Dolores said with a last touch of the comb.

104

"You look like a doll, Camilla. The boys will love you."

"Thank you," Camilla said. "Donna, could you go downstairs with Dolores and bring me back a Coke?"

"I'll have someone bring it up," Dolores said. A look passed between Camilla and Donna.

"We'll go," Donna said.

"I have something to tell you," Camilla said to Margaret when they had gone. "It's important." She looked excited, quite grown-up in her gown with her hair swept up.

"Yes?"

"I told Grandmummy that I'd do this party, but I didn't want to have any more parties or go to the coming-out balls this winter."

"And what did your grandmother say?"

"She was . . . she was angry." Camilla went to the dressing table and peered at herself in the mirror. "Do you think you'll marry Daddy? Grandmummy would like it. I wouldn't mind." She looked around at Margaret with a look that bordered on wistful pleading. She was waiting for the answer she wanted to hear.

"No. It's impossible," Margaret said gently. "Not that he isn't a nice person, but there's someone else I'm rather more interested in."

"Aunt Lynne said you and he might marry. Of course, she'd like to marry him herself. She's still young enough to have children, don't you think?"

"I imagine so."

"If Daddy got married again and had more children, people would worry about making them into the right kind of Staffords and leave me alone. It would be like starting over."

"Is that the important thing you had to tell me?"

"Oh no. After I told Grandmummy that I didn't want to go on with the debut, she . . . she bribed me."

"How clever of her," Margaret said, almost to herself.

"She promised to fix it so that I have a lot of my money right away, instead of waiting until I grow up. She runs the trusts, you know. Daddy only does the investments and things."

"A lot of money?" Margaret said. "What's a lot, if I may ask? In round numbers."

"Millions," Camilla said gleefully. "If I behave myself and go on with the plans."

"Does anyone else know?" Margaret asked.

"I told Donna about the bribe, but she'd never say anything. So I told Grandmummy I'd do it. Do you think it's wrong?"

"It's much easier to be independent if one is very wealthy," Margaret said. "But a lot of money is a responsibility for a young person to handle."

"You sound like Aunt Lynne. I need guidance, I need this, I need that."

"Lynne?"

"Well..." Camilla looked a bit shamefaced. "I mentioned it to her. But not to anyone else."

"Good," Margaret said. "It wasn't good, though, telling Lynne Jordan such things, even if she was your dead mother's sister."

Donna came back, and the mood of confidences was broken.

"Remember that this is a dress rehearsal for the winter balls," Margaret said brightly.

"But naturally. It will be too divine," Camilla drawled grandly, and the tone was too Lynne Jordan, too Eloise, too Society for words.

Margaret descended, pondering Eloise Stafford's bribe, and hoping she meant to carry it through if Camilla did her part.

Outside the house, all seemed to be in order. Bert Thurman was seen primping at the already perfect herbaceous borders. Rom stood guard at the porte cochere, awaiting the hired buses that would bring party-goers to the estate after they arrived on the hired railway cars. They were being chaperoned, as it were, by Paul. Even De Vere had half promised to appear, but she was not confident about that. He had not been enthusiastic. Nancy and Richie had been seen earlier, lounging beside the pool. Lynne was in an upper room, no doubt dressing to kill. Eloise was said to be gathering her strength in her wing of the house, in preparation for the onslaught of Society youth and the very select handful of her own friends who had been invited.

Margaret met Josef LeBaron on the lawn, where he was taking a final survey. Spacious pastel striped tents had been erected on the carefully tended lawns, which looked so much like three-hundred-year-old English grass that Margaret suspected some chemical artifice. No harm in that, as long as it did not cause foot problems among the young ladies who might choose to abandon high-heeled slippers after they had sunk into the turf a few times.

Huge blue, pink, yellow, and white helium-filled balloons floated above the tents, and lavish sprays of pastel blossoms hung in baskets above each table in the dining tent. Tiny pink and white lights were strung through the tents and over the dancing floor, ready to be turned on when the sun dropped closer to the horizon.

"It looks perfect," Margaret said.

"All that is required is money," Josef said. He straightened his understated, well-tailored blue blazer. "And exceptionally good taste. Would that fellow over there with the musicians be a guest or an intruder?"

Margaret turned and saw the shambling figure of Toby Stafford on the far side of the lawn. He was conversing with a cluster of musicians, some of them formally dressed string players, others underdressed members of the well-known (but not to Margaret) rock group Toby had insisted she engage.

"He's a guest," Margaret said. "Camilla's uncle, Toby Stafford."

"Not really! I remember him from the days when I was still handing around the canapés at cocktail parties at the Dakota. He used to be quite high fashion. Now he seems rather . . ."

"Eccentric," Margaret said. "We Brits are accustomed to that sort of thing in a family. You Americans are more inclined to pretend they don't exist."

"True enough," Josef said. "Oho! Grande Dame on the horizon. I'll disappear. It's your party now."

Margaret watched Eloise move purposefully in their direction, trailing lavender silk.

"It will be a perfectly lovely evening," Margaret said to reassure herself. She saw Josef bow graciously to Eloise and proceed briskly toward the safety of Manhattan.

"Margaret, dear," Eloise Stafford said. "Don't you look pretty. Blondes can look quite nice in that shade of rose." She was friendly again. "What a lovely job you've done, and quite without any supervision."

For a brief moment, Margaret wondered why the person who had murdered Ann Stafford hadn't had the good sense and possibly good taste to murder Eloise instead.

"Camilla is looking lovely, and even Donna is presentable," Eloise said. "A pity her father is unable to get about."

Suddenly a great joyous crowd of young people rounded the corner of the house and swooped down the lawn. There were so many of them, and most seemed to have taken to heart the invitation to don romantic evening dress. It had helped that Poppy Dill had done her bit to make the event worthy of consideration. An item in her "Social Scene" column a week before had prompted a sudden rush of acceptances:

> *Society's young set, back to the city from parts known and unknown, will be flocking next week to the fabulous Stafford estate in Cranford, Connecticut, for the first big party of the coming deb season. Lovely Camilla Stafford's evening by the sea promises to be divine, and her oldest and youngest friends are dying to enjoy the end-of-summer delights of one of the most beautiful summer homes remaining from the Good Old Days. . . .*

The young people seemed to know how to undertake their delights. Camilla in her flowing yellow gown was greeting them with considerable aplomb, looking like the Golden Girl of Long Island Sound. It was a relief to see Paul, elegance personified, strolling down the hill, and then to her delight, she saw De Vere.

"I never dreamed you'd be on the train," she said.

"It was due to Paul's persuasive pleading," De Vere said. "He mentioned the possibility of 'Uninvited Eurotrash.' I thought I should see them for myself."

Margaret said, "Paul, do we have Uninvited Eurotrash?"

"Those Spanish boys are in town, and some Italians. I know you can't trust the Italians. A boy named Sergio whom I have never thought well of. They always sense a party without being told. They are not responsible people, but they are fun-seekers." Paul's attention was captured by a pair of nubile wenches, one of whom was the daughter of the president of his bank's chief competitor in handing out vast sums to Third World dictators. He wandered off in pursuit.

"Everyone looks quite respectable," Margaret said. "Almost respectable."

There was a sharp blast of sound from the tent where the rock band had amassed a considerable amount of electronic equipment.

"Ah," said Margaret. "The rock band. 'The Scene As It Were,' or something of the sort. I didn't quite catch the name, but I understand they have a devoted following. Shall I introduce you to Camilla and her grandmother?"

De Vere nodded reluctantly. Paul had been captured by Nancy Stafford, backed by Richie whose blank expression slipped into gear when he caught sight of De Vere. Margaret thought she was not mistaken that he elbowed Nancy Stafford quite forcefully in her ribs, interrupting her chat with Paul. Nancy brushed Richie away with a flick of her well-tanned wrist.

"She will pay for that," Margaret murmured. "Richie seems to know you." Richie cast a glowering look at De Vere and slipped into the dining tent.

"I am constantly amazed at the follies of the upper classes," De Vere said. "I know that man, and I shudder to imagine the appeal he holds for the lady. If you insist on introducing me to the family, you might then spare the time for a dance. I choose the strings and piano over the rock group."

"This is my great friend Sam De Vere," Margaret said to Eloise. "De Vere, this is Camilla Stafford and her grandmother, Mrs. Stafford."

Eloise's handshake was firm, her smile was correct. She looked De Vere over closely and said with perfect cordiality, "How do you do? I was sure that my son Daniel would be Margaret's escort this evening."

De Vere ignored the quintessentially genteel rudeness of the remark and said, "What a pleasure to meet you, Mrs. Stafford." He turned to Camilla. "Thank you for allowing me to be at your party. I hope you'll save me a dance."

"Thank you for coming, Mr. De Vere," Camilla said, very poised now that the evening was well begun. "I'd like to dance with you."

"What is it that you do, Mr. De Vere?" Eloise said.

Margaret suspected she hoped that De Vere was something unspeakable, like an ax murderer or a defrocked stockbroker.

"The law," De Vere said. He smiled.

"Ah," Eloise said. She seemed to be trying to see him as a senior partner in a vast Park Avenue law firm and as serious competition for Daniel in capturing the heart and hand of Lady Margaret Priam.

"There's Daddy," Camilla said. "And Aunt Lynne."

Margaret had to admit to herself that Daniel Stafford knew how to make himself look good. Lynne was clinging to his arm, wearing a long white gown, girlishly demure and frothily ruffled. If only she weren't so painfully undernourished, she would be rather attractive.

"This is Daniel Stafford," Margaret said, "and Lynne Jordan."

The two men looked at each other warily. They shook hands, then both turned to Margaret.

"I see that Paul is signaling me," De Vere said. "I'll join you shortly, Margaret."

"Daniel," Eloise commanded. "Here's Hesketh Brooks. You know his father. Hesketh, I'm sure you remember Camilla. . . ." Daniel left Margaret reluctantly to greet a gangly youth with a thrust to his chin that denoted good, solid WASP genes.

Margaret looked about for a nice, soothing glass of champagne and found herself with Lynne instead.

"What an attractive man," Lynne said. Margaret thought that Lynne's perfect gloss was less than perfect tonight. The strain of competing for Daniel was beginning to tell on her, or perhaps the burden of knowing that her niece would soon command personal millions caused her to lose sleep. She seemed to have forgotten that a few days ago, she had been enraged with Margaret.

"Isn't he, though," Margaret said carefully, not liking to think of Lynne tangling with De Vere.

"Italian, I believe? I'm sure I've met him."

"You mean Paul." Margaret was relieved.

"Naturally, darling. He's surely a bit too young for you, but then . . ." She twittered a false little laugh. "He's probably even too young for me."

"You must know his mother. Carolyn Sue Hoopes."

"Not really! But he's so elegant, and I've actually seen Carolyn Sue in public when her bag and her shoes don't match."

"Doubtless Paul learned elegance from his father, the prince," Margaret said.

"And the other man?" Lynne tried to sound casual.

"An old friend," Margaret said.

Nancy Stafford lurched unbidden into the conversation. "That man you're with." She sounded somewhat the worse for pre-party intake of elevating substances. "Richie said he knew him."

To turn the conversation, Margaret said quickly, "New York is such a small town really. Josef LeBaron did a superb job for tonight, don't you think?"

But Nancy, if she cared, wasn't paying attention in any event. Nor was Lynne, who appeared to be surveying the increasingly dense throng intently, head erect and bony shoulders back. Margaret had a moment of pity for Daniel being so under the covetous eyes of his former sister-in-law.

"Ah," Lynne said. "Imagine that. Toby. How odd to see him at a civilized event."

"Where is my dear little brother?" Nancy swung her head around.

"There, by the drinks pavilion," Lynne said. "I suppose I ought to speak to him while I have the chance. I've heard of a quite nice group that could use some charitable funds. The kind of thing he's interested in."

"My brother doesn't have a generous bone in his body," Nancy said. "He just talks that way to annoy Mother and Daniel. But I love him." She swayed. "You always love your brothers. Toby used to be wonderful. Didn't give a damn about anything. He's so serious about things now."

"I ought to mingle," Margaret said, "to be sure everything is as decorous as it appears to be." She wanted to be free of these women, and since neither of them seemed to notice, she moved away. Nancy tottered in the direction of Daniel, and Lynne advanced on Toby to impart information on worthy recipients of Stafford money. Margaret paused. Or perhaps it was to inform him of his mother's crude but effective bribe that would diminish the Stafford trusts considerably.

The two musical groups were doing their jobs, although The Scene remained difficult for Margaret to comprehend. Couples were dancing to both, however, in the variety of ways that young people danced nowadays. The candles and the fairy lights glowed in the dusky evening. It was quite as she had hoped it would be, and she felt more confident that the whole process of Camilla's debut might work out after all. She found Donna nibbling a bit of finger food with a glass of something mild-looking in her hand.

"Are you having a good time?" Margaret asked.

"I guess so," Donna said. She shrugged and grinned. "Dad says it can't hurt to take advantage of your friends' advantages."

"He's missing a nice party." Margaret was still eager to speak to Matt, but had not determined how to arrange it.

"Yeah," Donna said noncommittally. "Your friend Paul is really cute."

"You'd have to be really rich to attract him, I'm sorry to say," Margaret said. "It's one of the funny things about him."

"Dad says we'll be rich someday. But not as rich as Camilla. She deserves what she's going to get."

"I wouldn't repeat that," Margaret said. "About Camilla getting something. You know what I mean." Donna wrinkled her nose. "Have a lovely time tonight," Margaret said. Donna glided off, handling her borrowed finery with grace.

Toby came silently up behind Margaret. "I'm not having a lovely time." He took her arm and guided her through clusters of eating, drinking, laughing youth. In spite of his affectation of shabbiness and his social renegade pose, to-night he was acting like the social Toby she had read about in the old clippings.

"Lynne said she knew of some charity that could use your help. I suppose you do a lot of that, but very few people know. At least I never see your name mentioned in the press. Most people like to have their good deeds shouted to the skies."

"There are always people who claim to need money more than I do," Toby said. "Lynne's one of them. You have to learn to distinguish between need and greed. And what I need is a drink," he said. "Not this cut-rate champagne. It's Daddy's decanters in the library for me. . . ." He ambled away.

Most of her duty had been done. The only thing left were the fireworks much later, to mark the party's end. It was time to find De Vere for their dance. She spied him engaged in conversation with a tiny, bejeweled old lady. Margaret couldn't imagine who she was, unless she was some great-great-aunt trotted out in a show of family support. Paul was enjoying a moment of glory on the dance floor, watched by usually blasé young women who had been turned to mush at the sight of him. He was fabulously handsome, Margaret thought, and when he got to be her age—say, thirty-five—and had found his place in life, he would be utterly devastating. Not unlike his father, Prince Aldo, whose comparative poverty had not in the least dimmed his glowing reputation as a ladykiller.

"Margaret." Daniel's voice at her back was soft and seductive. And quite urgent. "We need to talk."

"There's no problem, I hope."

"None that you can't solve," he said. "It appears that Lynne has been spreading rumors, and I want to clear them up."

Margaret looked longingly at De Vere.

"Would you know who that very old lady is?" she asked, postponing a tête-à-tête that was likely to be uncomfortable.

"The one talking to your lawyer friend?"

Margaret thought that news passed through this family almost too quickly.

"Yes," she said. She decided not to correct his impression of De Vere's profession.

"I have no idea. A party crasher perhaps."

She could find no graceful excuse to free herself from Daniel, and then she saw Lynne glaring at them from the drinks tent where a number of youths had commandeered their private bottle of champagne from a waiter and were filling their own glasses. A clutch of laughing girls came running shoeless down the lawn, their pale dresses floating about them.

Margaret thought things were going well.

Then she wondered if it was all too good to be true.

It was.

Chapter 11

Dusk settled rapidly on the Stafford estate. Long Island Sound slipped from blue to slate. The soft romantic sound of strings on the one hand and the muffled throb of the rock group on the other were not at all offensive to the ear.

One or two of the young party-goers seemed a bit the worse for wear, perhaps from the moderately good champagne that Toby despised.

Margaret was momentarily taken aback by the sight of a young man apparently disrobing at the bottom edge of the great lawn where the turf ended and the embankment above the sea began.

Daniel took a firm grip on her elbow and steered her uphill toward the house. Margaret saw Camilla in Leila's lovely gown standing at the doors of the solarium, backlit by the lamps that had been lighted inside. Margaret couldn't read her expression at that distance, but she seemed like a statue on display.

"Camilla is very like her mother," Daniel said. "A bystander."

"The innocent bystander," Margaret murmured.

"Ann had advanced beyond innocence," Daniel said. "Her attitude was reckless. As is Camilla's in some respects. Do you know that I'm jealous of your gentleman friend?"

"How flattering," Margaret said. In spite of herself, she reacted more than she would have expected to his nearness. A lot of money did create its own attraction, as Paul was always reminding her. What would her life be if, heaven

115

forbid, she decided to enter the Stafford family, live on Camilla's wealth? Live in that rarefied atmosphere above the common herd, above the law even.

They did not go to the big house. Daniel guided her to the right, toward the guest house and the old playhouse. Margaret hesitated. An attempted seduction in miniature surroundings was too silly to contemplate. But in that thought was the beginning of another: a place not visible from the main house was the perfect spot to meet a secret lover. Or someone who might kill in that same secrecy.

"I really ought to stay with the party," she said.

"Nonsense. Everything is going beautifully. Mother is pleased. The children are behaving, and there has been little damage to life or property so far. I want to show you something quite magical."

He took her down a flagstone path overhung by heavy branches so that it was like a dark tunnel. Then he rounded a corner and drew her through an archway carved through the hedge.

They were in an enclosed garden that Margaret had not seen before. It was filled with faint scents and an almost imperceptible rustle of leaves from the low flowering trees. Lights placed outside the tall trimmed boxwood hedge that surrounded the place cast a faint, pearly glow, so that one could make out the colors and shapes of the late summer flowers in their geometric beds. The tall cypresses Margaret had seen from the bridle trail stood at one end. In front of them was a marble bench flanked by tall white urns on classical pedestals, and overflowing with sprays of ivy and clusters of white flowers. In front of the bench, a slender jet of water rose and fell back with a delicate splash in the middle of a circular pool. Daniel's hand rested lightly on her shoulder.

"My father designed this garden especially for himself. He liked to sit here and meditate on the family fortunes, and how well his children and grandchildren would carry on."

"It's lovely," Margaret said. "Would this be the 'Italian garden'? The gardener mentioned such a place when we were doing the groundwork for the party, but I never saw it."

"Yes. Both my father and grandfather collected quite a few art objects in Europe. The statues were placed here."

He was walking her toward the bench, and Margaret sighed at what was surely to come: an exquisitely private romantic approach in an exquisitely maintained hideaway. She thought she could handle it, especially since it would give her the opportunity to put a stop to his interest in her. She was perfectly willing to leave Daniel Stafford to Lynne Jordan.

They reached the bench and sat to face the fountain. In recesses in the surrounding hedges, there were statues on low pedestals: an Aphrodite, a faun, a Roman bust. It was as though they were in another land at another time.

"Margaret, Lynne has told several people, quite spitefully and inaccurately, that she and I will marry one day. She feels that she has some kind of commitment from me, which is entirely untrue. I want you to know that my feelings for you are—"

Then the spell broke, and Daniel would not have a chance to utter silly pledges of deep and deepening affection for her.

Out of the darkening night, beyond the high walls that surrounded them, came a tremendous cry as though all the young voices gathered on the lawn shouted at once. Then with a magnificent crash, the sky lit up with an explosion of color and sound. Sprays of red and blue, expanding silver globes, showers of green, starbursts of white and gold, rockets of magenta, purple fountains filled the sky. Clouds of smoke, illuminated by the fireworks, rose to blot the stars.

Margaret stood up, afraid to imagine what might be happening.

"The fireworks so early?" Daniel asked.

"Far too early," she said. "Something is wrong. The fireworks were to come at the end."

She removed herself from the garden swiftly and with as much dignity as she could manage in the face of a minor disaster. She heard Daniel call, "Wait," but she did not pause and left him to follow at his leisure.

She found Paul hanging back at the edge of the crowd that applauded wildly and cheered as rockets flared and firecrackers exploded.

"What on earth happened?" she asked. "This wasn't what I'd planned."

"I will not swear to it," Paul said, "but I think Sergio, whom I mentioned earlier as being totally irresponsible, took it into his head to see a fireworks display immediately."

"Rom and Bert were to keep guard over the fireworks until the man arrived to set them off."

"I think they are not about. Is there great harm done?"

"No. As long as no one was injured. Where has De Vere got to?"

"Gone, I am sorry to report," Paul said. "He was called back to New York on this case he is working on. He could not find you. I did not say that you were last seen slipping into the foliage with Daniel Stafford."

"Damn." Margaret was greatly disappointed. "How did he leave? He came by train with you."

"The very old lady who was here, do you recall her?"

Margaret nodded.

"She, like Sergio, was not actually invited, but she read about the party in Miss Dill's column and decided she wished to attend. She told me that she had been to parties here in the old days. She had a car and driver, so De Vere went back to Manhattan with her. Richie was noticeably relieved at De Vere's sudden departure. Mrs. Jordan was not so pleased. She was asking Toby Stafford quite loudly where Daniel had gone. It is difficult to conduct a clandestine romance in the vicinity of the Staffords."

"Oh please, not you, too. I'll have to explain to De Vere why he couldn't find me."

"I will not ask you to explain to me," Paul said. "I understand the attraction of money."

"Emphatically not in this case," Margaret said. "I suppose I'd better locate Mrs. Stafford and apologize for the sudden fireworks."

She looked over the crowd, but she saw no Staffords, although Richie pushed his way through the throng of young people, glancing at them with some distaste.

"Jeez, that was something," he said. He did seem very much at ease. "You sure know how to throw a party. Great sight. I was up at the house when the fireworks went off."

"Were any of the family about?"

"Naw. Nancy went to lie down or something, so I was hanging around. I like that house, it's the kind of place I'd have if I settled down. Of course, I'd put in a sauna and fix up the billiards room. But I like all those matching books in the library, and all that marble. I really like marble. It's always cold, no matter what the weather is." He turned to Paul. "It's a taste that's born in you, right, *paisano*? You have any trouble with those kids, you let me know." Richie went about his business, a man relaxed now that the police had departed.

Margaret said, "I wonder where Mrs. Stafford is."

"I did see her going into the house earlier, before the fireworks," Paul admitted.

As the last hot cinders hissed out in the waters of Long Island Sound, the guests began to demonstrate their elevated spirits by dancing across the lawn. Shoes were abandoned, jackets flung on the grass. Very few people had actually disrobed completely, although one girl had apparently worn a bikini under her gown—surely those were not her undergarments—and was persuading a band of the more adventurous to follow her to the water for a nighttime swim. Several were disposed to follow her.

"I do hope they keep some garments on," Margaret said, "so there will be no complaints about the results of unleashed libidos."

But garments were dropping faster. A diaphanous chiffon here, a silky shift there. White jackets, blue blazers, grey trousers. The movement toward the sea became pronounced, and quite a bit of bare skin—young, tanned and healthy—was visible in the luminous lighting from the tents.

"It will be all right," Paul said. "They will swim, they will feel a chill, and they will retrieve their clothing."

"It was only to be expected," Margaret said. "Good work that it is nothing worse, although I doubt that Eloise will be amused."

"We need only worry that someone will be lost at sea, as it were, or otherwise damaged," Paul said.

"Someone should be watching over them. I don't suppose you have lifesaving credentials."

"I once effected a dramatic rescue in the Mediterranean," Paul said, "but it was more luck than intention. On the other hand, the young lady I rescued was wearing even less than Camilla's guests."

The gleeful shouts from the little beach indicated that no disasters were yet at hand. In the big house, lights were being turned on in all the rooms on the second and third floors, and even the topmost floor with its tiny gabled windows, and curtains were drawn.

A few of the less daring guests gathered decorously on the terrace outside the solarium.

"The Staffords are gone," Margaret said, "and the inmates are in charge of the asylum."

"They have not entirely vanished," Paul said. "That appears to be Nancy Stafford in a state of undress joining the others in the sea. No, now she seems to have changed her mind, although not her costume. . . ."

"I wish De Vere had stayed," Margaret said.

"He might have felt compelled to arrest them all," Paul said. "Still, I have seen groups of this nature behave in a far worse manner. Let me make my way toward the sea. I hope I don't have to plunge in. The waters in this part of the world are not warm."

Margaret ventured again in the direction of the house. Very few guests were now evident. If they weren't swimming near-naked in Long Island Sound, they were probably dallying in the bushes. Indeed, she stumbled across a pair of youthful cuddlers in the darkness, but they seemed to be behaving in a manner not likely to outrage common sensibilities.

"So sorry," Margaret said and moved on.

The rock music had ceased. A lone violinist played a plaintive rendition of "I Could Have Danced All Night," while the rest of the string players sat on the ground sharing the end of a bottle of champagne. They straightened up when they saw her, but she waved them back to their innocent pleasures. A group of surprisingly bosomy young women were packed onto a couch on the terrace, while two slightly drunken youths goggled at their cleavage and thighs and tried to sustain a conversation. Margaret left them alone.

She passed into the house. Since it had been made strictly off-limits to the guests, it remained untouched by the party and splendidly cold and impersonal. Dolores had been posted in a conspicuous spot near the staircase to wrestle to the ground any unwanted intruders.

"I am seeking Mrs. Stafford," Margaret said.

"I haven't seen her for hours," Dolores said. "She was being gracious to some old friend. Those were great fireworks."

"Thank you," Margaret said. "Not exactly as I had planned."

"Mrs. Jordan passed through a while ago before the fireworks," Dolores said. "She was looking like thunder and didn't even notice me. Toby went into the library earlier, but he's long gone. Richie was here, looking over the place as though he owned it. That's it for the Staffords, and their . . . their . . . And Richie."

Margaret let herself out the front door and stood under the porte cochere on the gravel drive. The cars of the family and their friends were parked close to the garage, and near them stood Rom with his back to the wall. He glowered as Margaret approached.

"I am looking for Mrs. Stafford," she said.

"Haven't seen her. She wouldn't be out around here anyhow."

"The other members of the family? Miss Camilla?"

"They'd be with the guests." Rom made them sound an unspeakable intrusion.

"Then I'll just look about a bit."

"No lights to speak of on the ground on this side of the house," he said. "You might get hurt." The prospect appeared to please him.

"I'll be all right," Margaret said. "I am accustomed to very large country estates."

She headed around the side of the garage, beyond which lay the tennis courts, the guest house, the playhouse, and the enclosed garden, and beyond them, the bridle trail. For a moment, Rom seemed prepared to halt her, but he hung back and merely watched her leave.

A faint glow lightened the night, perhaps from diffused starlight or the lights of the house. Margaret had no trouble finding her way along the path, although the dark shapes of outbuildings and the occasional decorative shrub were slightly disorienting. The entrance to the enclosed garden was a welcome landmark. It was not likely that Eloise Stafford would be contemplating the evening's affair in the serene garden, breathing in the flowery night scents, and planning future forays into the world of debutantes. Daniel would have long since departed.

Margaret might have passed by, but she heard voices coming toward her on the dark pathway, and so she ducked through the archway into the garden. She stayed close to the hedge to avoid being seen, and then backed into the recess that harbored a smooth, naked Aphrodite. The concealed lights that had showed the way earlier suddenly went off. No doubt Rom was punishing her.

"Not a bad little fete, I was afraid of the worst," a girl's voice drawled, "but that Camilla is *too* dreary. Mummy had a few choice words about the family, but she insisted I come. It's like a favor or something."

"Father has dealings with the Stafford man." The youth spoke with what Margaret had heard referred to as a prep school speech impediment. Something that tried to approach upper class English spoken through tightly clenched jaws.

"Shall we just duck in here for a second, Muffy?" The youth had discovered the entrance to the garden.

Margaret withdrew deeper into Aphrodite's embrasure. She didn't enjoy the prospect of being an unwilling witness to teenage gropings in the dark.

"Bobby, look! How divine! A secret garden."

Margaret slipped off her shoes. The grass beneath her feet was cool, and it was not uncomfortable to be standing hidden behind the statue's pedestal. In the darkness, Margaret could make out Muffy tripping lightly along the slate path with Bobby in pursuit. And yes, in a few steps, Bobby did manage to catch her and embrace her. Margaret plotted her escape while the couple was otherwise engaged. She picked up her shoes, ready to edge along the hedge to the entrance.

"No," Muffy said. "It's scary here. Too dark and mysterious. There are people in the shadows, I feel it." Margaret shrank back into the niche and held her breath while Muffy slipped from Bobby's arms and darted toward the entrance. Bobby pursued. Muffy halted at the entrance to the garden, and Bobby was allowed to capture her once again. Then they walked hand-in-hand out of the garden.

Margaret waited for the paths to clear. A cluster of chattering young people passed the garden but did not enter. Hidden behind Aphrodite, Margaret peered into the darkness of the garden. The cypresses at the back were outlined against the night sky. The fountain splashed. The breeze rustled the leaves. Suddenly alert, she stared toward the white bench and tall urns. Was someone moving stealthily in the shadows, or was the breeze ruffling the cascade of flowers and vines in the left urn? She waited. She did not want to be discovered in hiding by some romantically besotted pair of guests, nor did she want to discover them.

It was all so silly. Why was she bothering to rush about making apologies to Eloise Stafford? She could let the party run its course without her. If she waited long enough, whoever had slipped into the garden ahead of her and Muffy and Bobby would gather up their garments and depart. She sat down on the thick grass and leaned against Aphrodite's pedestal. Richie was right: marble was nice.

Margaret closed her eyes and half dozed.

When she came wide awake with a jerk, she couldn't tell what had aroused her. A sound perhaps. Then it came again: a brief, muffled thunk at the far end of the garden. Since she was sitting, her view was blocked by the lush planting along the path, so, very carefully, she stood and peered again into the scented darkness. The garden was silent. She heard no girlish giggles or masculine mutterings. She saw no movement.

She decided that the sound must have come from outside the garden: the careful closing of a car door perhaps. Or the distant explosion of one last firework. She stayed close to the hedge as she edged toward the garden's entrance. It would be wise to view the outer pathway carefully, lest Daniel appear and renew his attentions. She did not enjoy being forced to participate in the battle for the heart and hand of Daniel Stafford.

Margaret froze at the short, sharp ringing sound, as though someone had struck stone with metal. This did come from the back of the garden, and all Margaret wished to do was to depart immediately, whether Daniel was lurking or not.

As she reached the archway, she looked back. It was with utter surprise that she saw the huge, left-hand urn topple over and crash to the ground. She could feel the vibration under her feet as the tons of marble met the earth.

The pedestal stood empty like a decapitated soldier.

Her first thought was that she ought to tell someone, Rom or Bert. It was most dangerous to have an unstable statuary where someone might be hurt.

Then she saw a pale blur. A person ran out from the overhanging branches at the end of the garden and knelt on the grass where the urn had fallen beside the bench.

"No!" A high, terrified cry ripped through the night.

Margaret dropped her shoes and ran the length of the stone path to the garden's end.

"Camilla!" She pulled the girl to her feet. "Are you all right? What happened?"

Camilla trembled and pointed to the fallen urn, then she sobbed, "Look!"

Margaret closed her eyes quickly and opened them. There was something under the toppled urn. Someone.

I have to get Camilla out of here, Margaret thought. I must find help.

"Don't move, it will be all right," Margaret said, but she knew that it was not all right and would not be all right for the immediate future.

She looked behind them, around the garden. Except for the fountain, there was no sound at all. Nothing moved, but there were secret places in this secret place. Any of the niches might conceal a person.

Someone intent on playing a lethal game.

Margaret did not believe that huge marble urns fell over of their own accord.

Camilla seemed unable to move, although Margaret felt her shaking. Margaret took a brave step toward the fallen urn. She saw the carved marble, the earth and plants that had filled it spilled out onto the thick grass. She saw a bit of lacy skirt. An arm. A perfectly manicured hand. A splash of blood.

Lynne Jordan lay beneath a ton of stone. Once again, Camilla Stafford had come upon the body of a family member cruelly killed.

Chapter 12

"*I*t *was* a tragic accident," Eloise Stafford said with utter conviction. "I hold Lynne entirely to blame. She had no business roaming about in the dark." Eloise glanced at Margaret, another roamer in the dark, who had brought the ill tidings to Eloise, who had summoned the family immediately to a drawing room off the main hall, called a Dr. Morrison, and had sent a near-hysterical Camilla to bed under the care of Dolores and Donna Kessler.

"Prince Paul is kindly seeing to the dispersal of the guests. We intend to keep this very quiet," Eloise said.

Eloise did not seem distressed by Lynne Jordan's sudden and rather terrible death, although she had expressed a certain displeasure at the unfortunate manner with which Camilla's party had ended.

"It might have been more than an accident," Margaret began. "I believe the police should be informed."

"Nonsense," Eloise said. "We don't need any policemen. Besides, Dr. Morrison promised to call Freddie Beecher, the town constable. We've known him since he was a boy. That should be good enough."

Margaret tried again. "But I was right at the entrance to the garden when it happened. I saw..." The Staffords were looking intently at her. "I saw it happen," she said weakly. She decided to save her suspicions for someone who might actually listen, rather than these people who seemed intent on accidental death.

"I suppose this means the newspapers again," Nancy said yawning. "What a bore. God, I'm tired."

"There will be no newspaper stories this time," Eloise said.

"I don't think you're going to keep this entirely quiet," Margaret said. "You're a rather prominent family."

"I'll see to it," Daniel said shortly. "We'll be able to handle it."

"We always have," Toby said, almost with no hint of irony.

"Lynne was always foolhardy," Daniel said. "I told her the statues and urns in that garden were not secure. I told her thirty times if I told her once."

"You mean you lured poor Lynne out to your favorite trysting spot thirty times and never proposed?" Nancy said. "Shame on you."

"It was a figure of speech," Daniel said.

"Do you suppose our Lynne was lurking in the bushes waiting to see who Daniel was setting up for an amorous interlude?" Toby said. Margaret did not miss his glance in her direction.

"Toby," Daniel said, "I have put up with your uncalled-for snideness and viciousness and worse for years. I'll thank you to keep silent. You've done enough damage to this family."

Margaret was surprised by his genuine anger.

"Keep your temper, Daniel," Toby said coolly and strolled off to the baby grand at the opposite end of the room. He played Gershwin and Cole Porter very softly.

"I was elsewhere when the accident occurred. Speaking to Rom, actually. That's where Margaret found me." Daniel said. "In any case, Mother is right. It was an accident, and after we clear up the details tonight, that will be the end of it."

"But Camilla was there," Margaret said, then added quickly, "I mean she came into the garden somehow just after it happened, the way I did. This is a terrible thing for her."

"Camilla will be all right," Eloise said. "I'll have the doctor give her a tranquilizer."

"Look," Toby said. "This has shaken me up. I'm going upstairs to lie down."

"Don't disturb Camilla," Eloise said.

"I believe she may have to be disturbed," Paul said from the doorway. "There are two gentlemen on the grounds. One is a constable, the other a doctor. They are examining the . . . the scene. They have summoned an ambulance, and the constable wishes to speak to you shortly."

"I'm still going upstairs," Toby said. "Freddie Beecher knows where to find me. His father always managed to find me when anything went wrong in Cranford, and I guess Freddie is as good as his old man." Toby left the room.

"I suppose this will stop all the plans for the debut," Nancy said. "I was looking forward to it."

"I shouldn't think an accidental death in early September would have any impact on our arrangements for December," Eloise said. "It's not as if Lynne was much of anyone. We put up with her for Camilla's sake."

"Mother, you are delightfully heartless," Nancy said. "But you're right."

"I am. It would be a good idea if your . . . friend were not about."

"Richie left at the first smell of trouble," Nancy said.

"Good. I shall see Freddie. Prince Paul, if you could ask one of the maids to show him in." She gestured for all of them to depart. "I knew his father. His grandfather, if it comes to that. In the old days, when we had a nice group summering in Cranford, instead of these . . . renters, people one has never heard of." Eloise stood up, stern and in charge.

Margaret would have liked to stay, but they obediently left the room.

Daniel said, "Margaret, I cannot tell you how I regret . . ." He smiled sadly. "Mother has decided I should see Freddie as well, but as soon as we're finished . . ." He returned to the drawing room. An unknown maid was leading a lean and serious young man toward the portals of Eloise's lair.

"The constable," Paul whispered. "Doesn't look as though he could manage anything more serious than illegal parking."

"Hmm," Margaret said. "Quite different from constables back home. If Eloise has her way, it won't be anything more serious than illegal parking, even though I know there must be more."

Margaret stood in the middle of the great hall and stared up at the huge chandelier and the intricately painted ceiling. "What was Lynne doing alone in the garden?"

"She was not alone," Paul said. "Camilla was there. You were there."

"How did Camilla and Lynne get there? I know I dozed for a minute, and the lights were turned off. I saw the amorous teenagers, who quickly came and went. I heard sounds. But I didn't see Lynne come in—or the murderer."

"There was no murderer," Paul said.

"Then how did a very large piece of marble come to topple over just as she appeared? And if Lynne were alive and well when the urn tumbled, why didn't she just get out of the way?"

It was exactly the same puzzlement she felt about why Ann Stafford had not put up a fight or run away from an intruder in the solarium. The Harris girls of Fresno were surely not stupid.

Then she said, "Unless she was already dead."

"You are serious."

"I am," Margaret said. "But someone also pushed over that urn. Even if Daniel claims it was unsteady, I do not believe the Staffords would be so careless as to have unsteady urns on their property. I wonder where Bert is. He'd know the state of his gardens."

She looked longingly at the closed door to the drawing room. "I wish I could hear through walls. Now I should go up and speak to Camilla before anyone else does. Ho, Dolores."

The maid was halfway down the stairs.

"How is Camilla? And where's Bert, do you know?"

"He probably got into the booze and wandered off to the woods to take a nap. I hear the cops are here."

"The constable, a Mr. Beecher. He's speaking with Mrs. Stafford."

Dolores snickered. "Madame will eat him alive. He's only about two years older than me. We were at high school together. The Beechers always get elected constable in Cranford. Camilla's sleeping, and her girlfriend's up there with her. She's pretty shaken up. Maybe if you went and talked to her . . . Nobody from the family has bothered to come up." Dolores disappeared to the back of the house.

"I have to see her," Margaret said.

"Couldn't you leave it alone?" Paul said. "These Staffords will handle the situation as they see fit, with money or otherwise, and at least you need never again lunch with Mrs. Jordan."

"I can't leave it," Margaret said. "I have another thought. If someone pushed that urn on top of an alive Lynne, is it possible that she was mistaken for Camilla?"

Margaret started up the stairs.

"Margaret," Paul said. "Someone might have mistaken Lynne in her light-colored gown for Camilla in hers. But equally, someone might have mistaken Lynne Jordan for anyone. For you."

"How right! You are a detective in spite of yourself. See if you can locate Bert and Rom. Someone turned off the lights in the garden before I went in. Someone will know whether the statuary was unsteady."

Paul produced a gentlemanly shudder but obeyed. Margaret proceeded upstairs to find Camilla.

Who knew about Eloise's bribe and the planned transfer of funds to Camilla? Margaret wondered as she tried all the doors. She was never hesitant about opening closed doors.

Eloise knew, because she'd done the bribing. Donna knew, and probably therefore Matt Kessler knew. Lynne knew because Camilla had told her. Who might Lynne have told? She could have spoken to Daniel, Toby, and Nancy at any time that evening, and she wasn't one to keep secrets. Nancy might have told Richie. With the exception of Donna, Margaret could not see absolute innocence shining forth from any of them. Possibly Eloise . . . But Eloise might never have intended to keep her word about the money. And Eloise had Rom, a man with a questionable past, at her beck and call.

The first room Margaret tried was the one where Camilla had dressed, but a maid had already been there. There wasn't a trace of Camilla's preparations early in the evening, before the evening crashed.

The other doors—dozens of them—opened freely. Eloise's suite at the end of the hall was unmistakable: expensive and ladylike, beautiful furniture, orderly and fragrant. Some rooms were guest rooms for transients. One had obviously been Lynne's, full of Lynne-ish handsewn silk lingerie and hundreds-of-dollars-an-ounce Scents of the Moment on the dressing table. She opened a door on a comfortable man's room—Daniel's probably, since it seemed well lived-in with leather and brass and a master-of-the-house look. It was unlike Toby. No room on this floor harbored Camilla. At one end of the hall, a doorway opened on stairs that went up and down. It was too well carpeted to be the servants' passage, so it was likely the stairway to the upper floors.

On this floor the dark wood moldings around the doors were not so well polished, the wallpaper was not so tasteful, the rugs were somewhat worn. There were secondary guests rooms, a sewing room, and at the end of the corridor, above Eloise's suite, she found Camilla's own retreat. She saw a feminine touch in the small sitting room with flowered wallpaper and lacy ruffles. A few old dolls and stuffed animals, a photo of baby Camilla in her mother's arms gave it some life. Margaret picked up the photo: Ann Stafford had been quite beautiful, much more patrician-looking than Lynne.

In the adjoining bedroom, Camilla had been allowed to be a teenager. There were frills and flounces, but there were also posters of androgynous pop stars and faces from television and films that made girls' hearts beat faster. There was an expensive sound and video system, and a

case full of videocassettes and CDs. Camilla wanted for
nothing materially. Her gown was hung carefully on a
closet door, and the sandals she had worn were placed
neatly beside the bed. The bed was tumbled, a blanket was
tossed on a chaise. The two girls were not there.

"Camilla? Donna?" A faint hope lingered that one or
both would respond from the bathroom or closet or dressing room.

Silence. Where could they have gone?

"Camilla, please come out." Margaret heard the concern
in her own voice and hoped that Camilla would hear it as
well.

"She's gone." Donna came out of the bathroom,
changed into jeans and an oversize shirt.

"She can't be gone. The constable . . . the doctor. People
need to speak to her."

"About what? What could Freddie Beecher have to say
to her? And she's not sick, so why should she stay to see
the doctor?"

"It's the done thing when someone dies suddenly."

"Cam did that once. She didn't want to have to do it
again."

"All right then, where did she go?"

Donna assumed a look of bland innocence. "I don't
know," she said. "Honest. She said she wanted to get
away, so she went."

"Was she frightened? Did she say anything about . . .
about the accident?"

"That was awful, wasn't it?" Donna shuddered.

Margaret seriously wanted to shake her. "It might have
been Camilla who died under that piece of marble. Someone might have intended to push it over onto her instead of
Lynne."

"It was an accident," Donna said, but she was beginning
to weaken. "Dolores said so. Mrs. Stafford said so."

"Camilla must have had a reason for going to the garden."

Donna shook her head. "She never said. She was
around at the party. I saw her dancing with that cute prince

and some other guys. She was with me when the fireworks went off." Donna stopped, and Margaret waited. "She did say that she was going to find out something tonight once and for all. I don't know what she meant, and I'll never repeat that to anyone else." Donna was suddenly uneasy. "She was scared when we came up here."

"All right," Margaret said. "The important thing is to find Camilla. Would she have gone to hide in the play-house?"

"All she said was she had to get far away. She might have gone to her uncle Toby's place in New York. She did that once before."

"Do you know which Toby's room is?"

"It's upstairs on the top floor," Donna said. "He was here before Camilla left. He said she should call if she needed him. But she didn't. She left."

Margaret went up one more flight. When she pushed rudely into the big room, Toby was standing at the windows that faced out on the sound.

"Where has Camilla gone?"

Toby dropped the curtain and turned slowly. "She's gone? Beautiful."

"It's not beautiful," Margaret said angrily. "She might be in danger."

"My mother can be dangerous when a party of hers is spoiled by an ugly accident, but otherwise, what danger could there be?" He was smiling now, a thin, almost bitter smile. "That fool Lynne was creeping around in the bushes to see who Daniel was cozying up to." He continued to look at her. "As jealous as the day is long was our Lynne. Money, love, and her place in the social sun, that's what she wanted. Would Daniel have been cozying up to you, dear Lady Margaret, the way Mother planned it?"

"Certainly not!" Margaret said indignantly and not quite truthfully.

Toby lay down on his bed, propped up by a pile of pillows. "Have it your way," he said.

"Would she have a way to get to New York?" Margaret

asked. "Would she have gone to hide at your place in the city?"

"No," he said. "She knows I'd have to bring her back. She doesn't have any boyfriends I know of to hide her. Maybe the Kessler girl . . ."

"She's downstairs, professing ignorance of everything. How would Camilla have gotten out of the house?" Margaret asked. "Down the stairs and out the front door?"

"Not a chance. Rom or somebody would have seen her and stopped her. She probably took the back stairs at the other end of the hall, went out the servants' entrance, and off through the woods to town. She probably didn't borrow one of the cars. In town, she could pick up a late train to New York, or a late train to New Haven. Once you're in New Haven, you can catch a train to Boston. Or Hartford."

"Toby . . ." Margaret was again exasperated by this family. "I'm going downstairs."

"I'll join you, professing my own ignorance." He stood up. "I'd like to see you in action. You aristos are good at bluffing your way out of dangerous situations with the natives."

On the floor below, Margaret encountered massed Staffords, and the constable confronting Donna. Paul was an interested observer at the doorway. Donna was being coolly obstructive, shaking her head and wearing a semi-idiotic teenage expression that Margaret was certain was only a pose.

"Gee, Mr. Beecher, I don't know anything. Camilla said she wanted to get some air, so, like, she went out. She was real upset about her aunt."

"Lady Margaret," Eloise said imperiously. "Kindly explain my granddaughter's absence. Our constable feels he must speak to her before he can finish here. I want this matter closed as soon as possible."

Margaret and Paul exchanged a look.

"I can't explain anything, Mrs. Stafford." No more "dear Margarets" and "dear Eloises" in this relationship. "I came up to look in on Camilla, and Donna said she'd gone for a walk or upstairs to speak to her uncle."

"She didn't come to me, Mother," Toby said.

"I have sent Rom out to look around the grounds," Daniel said. "She won't have gone far."

"Then that's the end of it," Eloise said. "Freddie, there won't be any unnecessary trouble about this." It was not a question.

"As little inconvenience as possible, ma'am," the constable said.

"You will give my personal regards to your father. When Camilla has calmed down, I shall be happy to arrange for you to see her."

"Terrible thing to happen to a girl," Freddie Beecher said. "I remember Dad mentioning the other thing. . . ."

Margaret saw the wave of tenseness wash over the Staffords, then Eloise said lightly, "Accidents happen. One must learn to live with them."

The family relaxed.

"Well, then . . ." The constable was uneasy. "I got to see Doc Morrison and make sure everything is . . . taken care of."

"Then let us all go downstairs. I'm sure Rom has located Camilla by now, and the servants will be wanting to clean up and get to bed." Eloise led the way down.

Margaret hung back and turned to Donna. "Are you okay? Paul and I can take you home."

Donna shook her head. "My stepmother is picking me up. I called her. She's probably already waiting down the driveway."

"Close enough for Camilla to hop into the car and hide in the backseat?" Margaret asked.

"Oh, I don't think so," Donna said. "She's always had a getaway plan. I just don't know where she was going tonight."

"I see," Margaret said. "Perhaps we should leave now."

By the time Margaret, Paul, and Donna reached the great hall, Eloise was bidding farewell to Constable Beecher and another man who was likely the doctor. Outside the door, the flashing lights of an ambulance heading down the drive was visible. The party was over for Lynne Jordan.

"Has Camilla been found?" Margaret asked Daniel.

He shook his head. "Toby thought she might have found a way to go to New York and stay at his place. He's already left."

"Then Paul and I will walk Donna to Mrs. Kessler's car and be on our way ourselves. Please let me know about ◆Camilla."

"I will," Daniel said. "Margaret, I deeply regret this . . ."

"We'll talk," Margaret said.

Donna ran ahead, got into an idling car that then sped down the hill. Paul and Margaret walked to her car.

"Wait," Margaret said. Constable Beecher was writing something in the overhead light of his car.

"I'm Margaret Priam," she said. "I was rather in charge of this party."

"So Mrs. Stafford indicated. Sorry it turned out this way. Terrible kind of accident."

"I'm not sure it was," Margaret said. He looked at her as though she had taken leave of her senses. "I mean, will it be possible for whoever the doctor is to determine if she might have been already dead and lying on the ground when the urn fell on her?"

Constable Beecher winced. "It was an awful mess," he said. "You mean, she might have had a heart attack or something? That's an idea. I thought it was pretty strange that she didn't get out of the way, or at least try to."

"I thought I'd mention it," Margaret said.

"Thank you, ma'am. I'll keep it in mind. We'll be having a closer look at the accident site tomorrow when it's light." He concluded their conversation by turning off the overhead light and starting the engine. "Take care, now," he said. Margaret watched his taillights disappear down the drive.

Paul was leaning back dozing when Margaret started the engine of her car. She drove a short distance down the drive and rounded the first curve until they were hidden from the house.

"Why are we stopping?" Paul asked. "You are not going to do something foolish." But he said it without hope.

"Yes," Margaret said. "I want to look at the garden again and see whether Camilla was at the playhouse tonight. You stay here and turn aside anyone who might wonder why we are stopped."

"What could I say?" Paul asked desperately.

"You'll think of something. Say I forgot my bag at the house and couldn't turn on the drive so I walked back. I won't be long." She took a flashlight from the glove compartment. "Where are those shoes? Ah." Margaret dumped her party shoes in the back seat and retrieved comfortable Reeboks. "No time for glamour now."

She stayed close to the trees along the drive as she walked back. Before she reached the house, she found the service path that led behind the Italian garden, now easily identified by the tall cypresses that rose above the hedge. She planned to go around behind the garden and approach the entrance from the side away from the house, but as she came opposite the cypresses, she noticed a gap in the hedge. Moving carefully, she entered and found herself in a narrow passage. The back of the garden was a double row of boxwood, and rounding a corner, she found herself in the garden in back of and to the side of the marble bench between the urns. The old moon had risen and was casting a faint light, enough for Margaret to have a reasonable view of the garden. She held onto the flashlight she had brought from the car but did not turn it on yet.

The private way in explained how Camilla, Lynne, the murderer, and anyone one else could enter the garden without using the main entrance.

Lynne's body was gone, but the urn lay near where it had fallen. Margaret scanned the garden. No one was about. She listened. There were no sounds, except the perpetual fountain. Very slowly and carefully she edged along behind the bench to the empty pedestal. Shielding her light, she turned it on the pedestal. She couldn't tell pre-

cisely, but it seemed to her that the spot where the base of
the urn had rested was chipped, as though someone had
contrived to loosen the huge object from its foundations.

One of them did it, she kept thinking, and it could have
been any one of them. And why Lynne, if indeed Lynne
was the intended victim?

A little braver now, she walked to the spot where Lynne
had been crushed. The grass was flattened, and there was a
noticeable depression in the ground from the force of the
urn toppling over onto Lynne.

If Lynne had already been lying there unconscious or
dead . . .

Margaret looked down at the spot. Then she looked
again. Under the thick and matted grass, she saw a dot of
white. Swiftly she picked it up—a tiny ball of tissue paper
wrapped around a hard object.

In another second she was into the passageway behind
the garden and out onto the service path, breathing hard.
She clutched the ball of paper as she hurried on, keeping to
the shadows and stumbling only once.

The playhouse was dark, the doors were locked. But
Margaret shined her torch through the window of the back
door to the little kitchen, and saw that the bottom drawer
that had held the box of treasures was open.

The box was gone, gone with Camilla to whatever ref-
uge she thought was safest.

"I thought you would not return alive," Paul said
crossly. "No one came near the car, but I kept imagining
people lurking in the underbrush. Did you accomplish anything?"

"No," Margaret said. Paul would say something tiresome about concealing evidence if she told him about the
ball of tissue paper. She wanted to be home before she
looked to see what it held. "No Camilla about."

They drove back to Manhattan without speaking much.
She left Paul downtown in Chelsea and reached her building not long after midnight.

Somehow she was not surprised to see Camilla asleep in
one of the uncomfortable but decorative sofas in the lobby,

under the watchful eye of the night doorman.

"I told her she could wait," the doorman said, "since she seemed to be all right." "All right" to the doorman meant not one of the city's tribe of homeless, drug-addicted, or obviously insane.

"Come along," Margaret said when she had nudged Camilla awake. "We have to talk, and I have to let your family know where you are."

Camilla was clutching her box of treasures from the playhouse.

"I won't go back," she said. "I'm scared."

"Scared of whom?"

"I don't know," Camilla said. She walked around Margaret's apartment, looking at the photos in silver frames and the paintings on the walls. She was working up to say something.

"Did you see something? Hear something?"

"No," she said too quickly.

"You came in through the back entrance, didn't you? And you did see something, or someone. Was it someone you knew?"

"No!" she said again. "I mean, I saw Aunt Lynne go into the garden by the back way, and I waited for a minute. I . . . I heard people whispering, I think, but I was behind the hedge so I don't know for sure."

"Then someone else was there. Why didn't I notice? Wait. I dozed off, so someone else could have come in the back way before Lynne did. Even if I were wide awake, it was too dark to see anything much." Margaret shut her eyes tight and tried to remember clearly. She had noticed some movement that she had taken to be branches stirred by the breeze. Then she had been awakened by a sound.

"Did you hear anything else?" Margaret asked.

"There was a sort of noise," Camilla said hesitantly. "A thump, two thumps. That's when I came along the passageway and looked into the garden."

"How long did it take you?"

"To reach the garden? Not long. A few seconds," Camilla said. But Margaret thought that was long enough for someone to dart behind the massive pedestal.

"And then you heard a sharp noise."

Camilla's frightened look told Margaret she was right.

"And then?" Margaret held her breath, as Camilla struggled to decide what to say. "Why didn't you call out to her when the urn began to topple over?"

It was almost a relief when Camilla said finally, "Margaret, Aunt Lynne wasn't standing near that urn. She was already lying on the ground when I reached the back way into the garden. I don't know whether she was dead then, but she wasn't moving. I didn't see anyone, but I heard the noise just when I was going to go to her, and then the urn—" Camilla caught her breath, seeing the horror again in her mind.

"Why were you there? You must tell me."

"I was following her," Camilla said softly. "I heard her say something to Aunt Nancy. Something like, 'I've never gotten justice from this family, but I will tonight. One little conversation will do it.' Then after a while, she started, you know, edging away from the party, so I followed her. I don't know who did it, and I'll never tell anyone what I told you, ever. Please, do I have to go back?"

"Not tonight," Margaret said, "but I have to let them know. And Camilla," she added, in the futile hope of calming her, "we don't know that someone actually killed Lynne. All we know is that she was on the ground. Maybe she fainted or had too much champagne. Maybe what you thought were whispers were the leaves rustling. Maybe it was just an accident that the urn fell. . . ."

"Maybe," Camilla said in a tiny voice. But Margaret knew they were both wondering where all the Staffords were when Lynne died, where was Richie, where was Rom? Were there others about who found Lynne Jordan disagreeable enough to kill?

She sent Camilla to bed with her treasure box, without the questions being asked aloud.

When Margaret rang the Stafford house in Connecticut, there was no answer. There was no answer at Toby's apartment downtown, but she left a message on his answering machine.

"Stupid," Margaret said to herself. She dialed the Kesslers' number. A sleepy woman answered, the new Mrs. Kessler.

"I've tried to reach the Staffords," Margaret said, "to tell them that Camilla is here in New York with me. They don't answer. I thought someone in Cranford ought to know."

"Donna figured that's where she'd gone," Mrs. Kessler said. "I'll call Freddie Beecher and let him get in touch with them."

"She's scared," Margaret said.

"I don't blame her," Mrs. Kessler said. "Eloise Stafford is enough to scare anyone."

Margaret unwrapped the twist of tissue. Inside was a little silver pendant with the letters *A* and *D* engraved on it.

A clue at last. Although Margaret could imagine what the initials signified, she did not know the significance of the trinket that had witnessed Lynne Jordan's end.

Chapter 13

If the Staffords hoped to keep Lynne Jordan's demise a family secret, they were disappointed. It was not quite front-page material, but it rated a story in the morning tabloids, in part because of the way she died. Being done in by a large marble urn ("imported") was colorful in a ghastly sort of way. The words "tragic accident" took on more sinister implications when mentioned in connection with Ann's unsolved murder. Margaret winced to see her own name mentioned as "first on the scene" and "discoverer of the body." De Vere would be furious.

As indeed he was, when he called her very early.

"I'm afraid it was murder," she said, "but it wasn't my fault that I was there."

"It wasn't murder," De Vere said. "I spoke to the town constable's office. There was no evidence of foul play."

"Mmm," Margaret said. She looked at the little pendant in the palm of her hand. "De Vere, Camilla swears that she saw Lynne Jordan lying on the grass, unconscious or dead, before the urn fell."

"Then Camilla ought to tell the authorities. If it's true."

"Why would she lie? And she can't—she thinks someone in her family is responsible, and you can't tell a seventeen-year-old that she has to turn in a relative."

"Do you suppose Lynne Jordan might have sipped a bit too much champagne, and wandered off to some quiet spot, stretched out on the grass. . . ."

"You don't believe that," Margaret said.

"I wish you would sever your connections with this family," De Vere said.

"I'm afraid I can't quite yet," Margaret said, as Camilla trailed into the living room. "Camilla ran away last night and ended up at my flat."

"Return her at once." De Vere sounded rather angry. "I don't doubt that the Staffords will accuse you of kidnapping her."

"But, De Vere . . ."

"She's a minor, and nobody's going to allow you to harbor her. They'll be there to get her, and there's nothing you can do about it."

"You are so damned cold-blooded," Margaret said, now angry herself. "She's a scared kid."

"If you think there's a murder involved, which there is not according to the people in charge, then you ought to speak to someone."

"I am," Margaret said. "I'm speaking to you."

"I have told you what I thought. You are being stubborn and perverse about this. You people think you can get away with murder."

"That's exactly what I've been saying," Margaret said. "You're right. I have to go now." She hung up.

Camilla in her runaway's jeans and shirt looked very little like the poised near-deb of the night before.

Margaret tried to put De Vere out of her mind. "I'm going to have to call your grandmother," Margaret said. "Then we'll get breakfast." Before any of that could be undertaken, however, the telephone rang.

"Lady Margaret." Eloise's voice was icy. "I understand that my granddaughter is with you. We have spent a frantic night—"

"I telephoned your house, I left a message on Toby's answering machine, and I spoke to Mrs. Kessler."

"Daniel has already left to pick her up. I trust that she will be there and ready to leave."

"She'll be here," Margaret said. Camilla looked stricken.

"I want to stay here," she whispered. "Please."

Margaret shook her head sadly as she listened to a few more choice words from Eloise. Then she became annoyed. "Under no circumstances did I encourage Camilla to come here. She is free to stay as far as I'm concerned."

"Please let me speak to Camilla," Eloise said. Margaret handed Camilla the receiver. Whatever her grandmother said to her, Camilla merely nodded forlornly.

"Yes, Grandmummy," she said finally. "I was just upset about Aunt Lynne. Yes, I will be good." She hung up. "I have to go back."

"I see," Margaret said. "Do you want to tell me what your grandmother said just now?"

"Oh, she changed the rules," Camilla said bitterly. "Now it's not that if I do the debut she'll let me have the money. Now I have to do exactly what she says. Exactly."

"I see," Margaret said. "I probably won't be helping with your debut after all. Your grandmother was quite angry with me."

"Please," Camilla said. "You're the only one I can trust."

"Nonsense. They'll find some nice lady who knows far more about making debuts than I do, and she'll help you through everything. It will be fine."

"Could I leave my box of things here with you for a while?" Camilla asked. "I don't want them to find it."

"You can put the box in that drawer. It will be safe." Margaret wanted to ask her where the little objects had come from. What kind of older and happier memories did they hold?

"I suppose you want to know what's in the box," Camilla said. She opened it. "The pen was Mummy's. She kept it in the playhouse. This was an old ring that belonged to my grandmother. Not the Stafford one, but Mummy's mother. The miniature used to be in the big house. It was supposed to have been stolen when Mummy was killed, but I found it in the playhouse. It was hidden in one of the drawers."

"Maybe your mother liked to look at it."

"I found the chain in the playhouse, too. Mummy used

to wear it, but . . . but it must have broken and got lost in the furniture."

There was no time now to ask about the pendant. The buzzer from the doorman downstairs rang. He announced that Mr. Stafford was waiting in the lobby to fetch his daughter. He did not wish to come up.

"I'll go down with you," Margaret said. "You can call me anytime you want to. You can always come to me if anything happens. Dolores Wisniewski is your friend, too."

When the elevator doors opened onto the lobby and she and Camilla emerged, they were greeted not by Daniel alone, but also by Nancy and Toby.

This is not unlike a poorly contrived Gothic novel, Margaret thought. Aloud she said, "I'm so sorry I couldn't reach any of you last night to tell you Camilla was here. I thought since Toby came back last night, he at least would have my message."

"I didn't play my messages," Toby said.

How odd, Margaret thought, considering that he was on a mission to find his niece who might well have phoned him.

"We're going to take Camilla away for a little holiday," Daniel said, "as soon as everything is taken care of. The funeral is the day after tomorrow. Lynne had no other family, except for her former husband. We want to do what's best for her."

He sounded so sincere, Margaret almost believed him.

"Then there will be no further investigation?" Margaret asked.

"Investigation?" Daniel strained to look puzzled.

"About Lynne's death. I thought that in the case of accidental death . . ."

"Mother feels that quite enough has been done," Daniel said. And that was the end of it.

"Mother was really annoyed with Camilla for running away," Nancy said, "but not with you, Margaret. We'll have lunch soon, shall we?"

"I'll call you when we get back," Daniel said. He put a

fatherly arm around Camilla's shoulders. "You're a big, brave girl," he said to his nearly grown-up daughter. "You have to learn to deal with this kind of senseless tragedy."

Margaret looked at Camilla's wan face and hoped she was not turning her over to a pack of bloodthirsty murderers.

There was no mention of the further plans for the debut.

When Margaret reentered her apartment after watching the Staffords herd Camilla into the waiting car chauffeured by Rom, her phone was ringing wildly, as though to convey the frantic excitement of Poppy Dill who was on the other end of the line.

"Tell me absolutely everything! This is sensational! Now maybe it will come out how Lynne managed to live so well merely on Philip's alimony, which isn't that much, a pittance compared to what she would need to live the way she did. I mean, a few free evening dresses are all well and good, and I never wanted to say a word before this because I loathe unfounded gossip, but there must have been some rich lover keeping her—"

"Poppy," Margaret managed to get in. "There's nothing to tell. A terrible accident."

"It's surprising how few people liked Lynne really," Poppy said. "Except for the fact that she moved in the right circles, and she knew a lot of the right people, she was nobody's best friend for more than ten minutes. All right, tell me what happened."

Margaret thought quickly, deciding what position she would take with Poppy. It would do Camilla no good to say to someone like Poppy that probably a family member did Lynne in, and Ann as well. "It was an accident. Lynne was in the wrong place at the wrong time. I think she believed that Daniel and I were together in this private little garden, and she crept in to eavesdrop. Well, we weren't there, but somehow a huge urn fell over and killed her."

Poppy's sniff of disbelief was clearly audible.

"You upper-class English girls are such innocents."

"What do you mean?"

"I mean that terrible things keep happening out there.

I'd advise you to take care of yourself and to stick close to the poor girl."

"I don't think the Staffords are going to continue to have me guiding Camilla through the intricacies of the debut."

"Nonsense," Poppy said. "They need you more than ever. Keep your eyes and ears open."

Margaret promised.

Then she tried making a list based on who was reported to have been in Cranford the day Ann Stafford died four years ago and who was at the party.

No one but Matt Kessler was likely to have been there four years ago, and he was the only one who was not at the party.

One more try at Matt, she thought. And if I talk to Bert Thurman, I can find out something about the state of the marble urns and statues in that garden.

The day of Lynne's funeral service seemed the only opportunity she'd have to venture to Connecticut without encountering a Stafford. They'd all be at Campbell's, along with all those friends of Lynne's who didn't really like her, to bid adieu to the thinnest of them all.

Chapter 14

*T*he *Stafford* house in Cranford was shut. Not simply empty for the day, but closed for the season, stripped of inhabitants, sheeted and shuttered. The gardener's shed was padlocked. The fountain in the Italian garden was drained and silent. The murderous urn had been set upright but had not yet been replaced on its pedestal. In front of the house, not a trace of the party only three days before remained. The curtains were drawn on every window, the outdoor furniture on the terrace was gone. The swimming pool beside the guest house was drained and covered.

It was eerie to walk the grounds in total silence on a warm day shortly before the coming of fall. The roses in the gardens were beginning to drop their petals, the purple asters and golden chrysanthemums were coming into their own, but it looked as though no Staffords would be there to see them. Perhaps they would never return. After three or four Stafford generations in this extravagant house, the property would fall into the hands of Matt Kessler or the like and be subdivided into respectable plots for the newly affluent who yearned for a summer retreat beside the sea.

Margaret took a last look at Long Island Sound. It seemed a different, deeper blue than it had earlier in the summer. Autumn blue. She returned to her car, half hoping that Bert would emerge from some forest grove or from behind a high hedge. He did not.

Margaret went on down the drive to take care of other business in Cranford.

There was only one Wisniewski family.

"She's upstairs packing for school," Dolores's mother said suspiciously. "You from the big house?"

"I met her when she was working for the Staffords," Margaret said. "I need to ask her a question."

"They're no good," Dolores's mother said. "Everybody in Cranford knows that, no matter how rich they are. The one that got herself killed, the first one." Mrs. Wisniewski sounded as though multiple violent deaths were only to be expected among the wealthy. "I always said she was sleeping with anybody who asked, same as the sister Nancy. And that Toby. Used to raise hell every summer when he was a kid. And Daniel . . ."

"What about him?"

Mrs. Wisniewski eyed her cagily. "I shouldn't be spreading rumors. Well, he and the wife used to have terrible fights. He had plenty of girlfriends, to hear people talk."

"Hey, Ma. You listen to too much gossip." Dolores came into the kitchen. "Lady Margaret, what can I do for you?"

"The Stafford house. It's all closed up."

"We worked like crazy people to get it done in two days. Madame told us to go to work at it the morning after the party, and we did. They brought some extra help in. Packed everything. Say, is Camilla okay? I heard she ran away, and they brought her back. She looked lousy. Terrible thing to have happen." Dolores shrugged. "As long as they only kill off each other. She's a good kid. I'd hate to have anything happen to her."

"And I," Margaret said. "Would you know where I could find Bert Thurman? I couldn't find anyone by that name in the telephone directory."

"He's not from around here," Mrs. Wisniewski volunteered. "From upstate. He had a room at Milly Black's boardinghouse. She keeps rooms for summer people. Bert came down this last spring to work for the Staffords."

"He left early this morning," Dolores said. "I saw him driving off."

"Off to where?"

"I forget. Someplace near Waterbury. What do you need him for?"

"I wanted to ask him about the urn. It didn't seem likely that Bert would allow a dangerously unsteady thing like that in a garden under his care."

Dolores and her mother exchanged an uneasy look.

"Well . . ." Dolores said reluctantly. "I didn't exactly ask him anything, but he was real nervous the past couple days. I thought if I had to cross-examine him, I'd try to find out why. But I have a pretty good idea. I'd say he knew somebody had done something to that urn so it could be tipped over without any trouble. I don't know if you could guarantee that it would crush the life out of a lady, but it sure as hell would scare her."

"Is there any way I could locate him?"

Dolores shook her head. "Awful lot of little towns tucked away in the Litchfield Hills. It's kinda out of the mainstream."

Mrs. Wisniewski cleared her throat. "Milly'd know. She's not one to let folks stay at her place without knowing where to send the bill if they run out on her."

"She's right off Main Street," Dolores said.

"Thanks," Margaret said. "If I ever need a good lawyer . . ."

Dolores laughed. "I was thinking of going into corporate law. Criminal law means you have to deal with the likes of the Staffords. You see that Camilla comes out of this okay."

"The last I heard," Margaret said, "she was going to be very, very wealthy as soon as her debut was over."

"Is that right? That would mean a lot less for the rest of them, and they sure like to spend money. Nancy and her cocaine and boyfriends, the good life for the father. All those country houses and city houses. And Toby always asking Mr. Daniel and his mother for more money. I've got to laugh about him. He was as high and mighty as the rest of them, no matter how many patches he put on the elbows of his Pierre Cardin jackets. Look, you won't repeat anything . . . I mean, nobody's going to put me on a witness stand about this."

Margaret found Milly Black, a diminutive lady in a rather bad wig, who told her the name of the town in up-state Connecticut that Bert hailed from.

"But don't go bothering to chase after him," she said. "He showed me a plane ticket. He was heading for Hartford to take a plane to California. The Staffords got him some kind of fancy gardening job at a big hotel out there." But Milly had no idea where. California was just a big state right before the end of the world.

"He paid me what he owed me in cash," Millie said. "With a little extra. Said he wouldn't be back next year."

Margaret sighed.

"The Staffords do that kind of thing," Milly added. "Last time somebody died up there, the one who was murdered, they did the same thing. Found all the servants new jobs, gave them plane tickets and a handful of cash. My, but it's nice to be rich."

Margaret didn't think it was nice at all, if that was what riches were used for.

All that was left for her to do in Cranford was to beg, plead, and cajole—bribe if necessary—to speak to Matt Kessler. He had once had something to say to her, before he was frightened off. Maybe he would say it now.

The second Mrs. Kessler was not what Margaret expected. She was not a dishy dame, but a petite brunette with a pageboy, well-tanned and relaxed, except when it came to her husband.

"Matt's mentioned you," Linda Kessler said. "After his accident, he didn't want to have anything more to do with the Staffords. I had to let Donna go to the party, and if the debut comes off this winter, I'll never hear the end of it if I don't let her go to that. And I do like Camilla. She's a straight kid."

"Could I speak to Matt?"

Linda Kessler looked surprised. "Of course. Wasn't he at the office?"

"I didn't stop to see. The Staffords implied that he was still bedridden."

"Not at all. He takes a cane along in case the leg gets tired when he's showing houses, but he's okay. The Staffords helped out with the medical expenses."

"Did they indeed?"

"You know," Linda said, "I only met and married Matt long after that terrible thing with Camilla's mother. He won't talk about those days, but Donna told me once that she felt guilty because she let Camilla go home alone and find her mother." Linda looked Margaret straight in the eye. "I've always thought that Matt was having an affair with Ann Stafford. He never told me, but I know it. I think that's why his first wife left him. He used to be really in love with those rich society people. I don't think he had anything to do with her death, but I think he knows or suspects something, and the Staffords have been paying him off for his silence." She looked at the wide gold wedding ring she wore. "And I think one of them tried to kill him back in August. There was another car."

"For that matter, they sort of tried to get rid of me," Margaret said. She was almost cheerful. Finally she might get some answers.

Matt Kessler looked up from his desk and smiled ruefully. "I wondered how long it would be before you turned up."

"You haven't made it easy for us to talk," Margaret said.

"Hey, I was attacked while innocently on my way to see you."

"Attacked by whom?"

"I was forced off the road from behind. It could have been the Stafford Mercedes, the one Dan drives, but I can't be sure. I was too busy trying to keep control. I couldn't tell you who was driving. It could have been anyone: man, woman, the cook, the gardener, the chauffeur, even that thug Richie. When I came to, I didn't want anyone to know I had any memories. I still have my eye on more

Stafford property. They'll have to sell sooner or later, and they'll have to sell to me. I want a lot of good things for Donna and Linda."

"Matt, who killed Ann Stafford four years ago?"

Matt shook his head. "Ann had someone, some man who was in love with her. She was going to drop him. She had a lot of men over the years I knew her. Daniel wasn't faithful, you know. She had to find some way to keep herself sane in that family." Matt took a deep breath. "I'm not excusing her. I was one of them. That was what I wanted to tell you back this summer, the day of the accident. I wanted to explain about Ann and me. It helped break up my first marriage. The thing with Ann didn't last, and it was over long before she died, but we sort of stayed friends. Anyhow, she dropped me the way she was going to drop this other guy. I don't know who killed Ann, but if you ever find out who she was having an affair with . . ." He looked down at the floor, unable to meet her eye.

"Matt, could I ask you—where did you and Ann meet? Not in public, surely." Margaret thought she knew the answer.

He looked sheepish. "That old playhouse."

"Ah. I see. And the others, as well, I presume."

"It's easy enough to get there privately, if you know the way. There are trails through what's now Cranford Hills. You come right off the road, onto the Stafford property."

"And now someone has murdered Lynne Jordan."

"What?" Matt was genuinely surprised. "It wasn't an accident? Donna said it was." He shrugged. "I ought to know that anything's possible with the Staffords. Look at me. But what kind of proof do you have?"

"My intuition, my eyes, and a curious tale told—" She decided to keep Camilla out of it. "Told by someone rather convincing. I suggested to Mr. Beecher that he try to determine if Lynne were already dead before the urn fell on her," Margaret said, "but he didn't appear eager to pursue that."

He thought for a minute. "No, he wouldn't be eager to do something that would displease Eloise. A lot of the town feels it has to regard them as though they were just a little above the ordinary law." He almost grinned. "Not too many rabid reformers in Cranford yet." Matt Kessler's grin disappeared. "Are you saying that Lynne maybe suspected who killed her sister and was shut up for good? You mean one of the Staffords?"

"Maybe. And maybe it was more than suspicion. Perhaps it was knowing with certainly—and with proof. Would you know . . . ?"

Matt put up his hands. "Look what knowing things got me. Nearly a trip to the cemetery. Sure, I think they thought I knew more than I did about Ann's death, and they tried paying me for my silence. When they found out I was meeting you, they decided to do something more."

"And whoever ran you down also tried to scare me or get rid of me." She told him about the tumbling log. "It was a rather feeble attempt, but still . . ." She stood up, then stopped at the door. "I found a note in the playhouse, probably written to Ann. It said, 'You will be in danger.' I wonder who wrote it?"

Matt looked at her. "Not I, but Ann got a note like that the summer she was killed. She even called to ask me about it. I remember because she also told me she was considering a divorce, that she was fed up with feeling like an outsider."

"Did she explain why she was finally considering a divorce after all those years?"

"She didn't say. We weren't that friendly. But she was worried about Eloise's reaction and losing Camilla. She really loved Camilla, but she was going through a sticky patch with her, teenage rebellion and that stuff. Camilla probably sensed trouble and was siding with her daddy. I went through that with my own kid. You take care of yourself."

"I will," Margaret said. "By the way, I think you ought to explain about Ann Stafford to your wife." When Matt started to protest, she added, "Besides, she already knows, but she'd rather hear it from you."

Chapter 15

A totally dead end, as far as Margaret could determine. She sat in her apartment and pondered the little silver pendant. The *A* and the *D* could only be Ann and Daniel, a token of a happier time that had somehow reached Lynne's hands. She had never had a chance to ask Camilla about it. Now, not only was the Connecticut house closed and the servants dispersed, the Staffords themselves had vanished. The staff at the New York house would give no information.

She had a number of invitations, now that the social season was beginning its autumn dance, but she felt depressed and lethargic. Paul, who was always a tonic, was happily being torn to pieces by three gorgeous, rich young women: Jytte the Scandinavian, who had decided that a few more weeks at the Plaza-Athénée couldn't hurt; Nina Parlons, who had returned to the city and was still testing Paul's suitability for an heiress of the Pacific Northwest; and finally Leila Parkins, who had suddenly revived her mild interest in Paul's princely title and other attributes.

Sadly there was no De Vere. He had not spoken to her since their last, angry phone call. Paul had not been forthcoming about his roommate's activities: "Very busy. Serious crime prevails in this city. I do not know why anyone lives here, except me because I am required to."

She wanted to ask if he thought De Vere was seeing someone else. Not that she was jealous. She understood that he was from a different kind of world, had different kinds of friends and interests, and didn't approve at all of

her society connections and activities. He wasn't "hers"—
of course not. She wasn't hurt and unhappy. Not at all. But
for a brief moment, she was furiously angry that he could
share so much with her and then turn aside as though it
didn't matter.

Angry.

Margaret stood up suddenly. She had slipped for a second into the trap of the well-born, assuming that there was
an unspoken right of a certain class to possess and control
the lives of others.

"I understand," she said aloud, "but I will never prove
it." Her anger faded. She telephoned Paul at the bank.

"Has De Vere mentioned anything about this thing with
the Staffords?"

"No," Paul said cautiously. "Although he did claim to
be irritated by your dangerous curiosity, as though . . ."

"What?"

"You took it as your right to interfere. Of course, he
does not believe that there has been a murder."

"There was, but we'll leave that for the moment. The
Stafford interlude is over, and I can think of no way of
proving who did what to whom. Kasparian is due back
tomorrow, and I shall return to the antique shop. I believe
you should persuade your mother to fly in to spend many
thousands on some precious treasure from the East. Jade,
ivory, porcelain from China, say."

"She is to arrive here soon for a visit, now that the
summer is over," Paul said. "But her idea of a treasure
from the East is a trunkful of unneeded garments purchased
in New York. I am not altogether sure she knows where
China is."

"Carolyn Sue has a very good idea of where everything
is. She is merely selective about expressing knowledge,
depending on the circumstances."

"I see that my personal vice president is signaling me,"
Paul said from his neat and seldom overworked desk at
United National. "If you'll forgive me for ringing off. I
find it alarming when he takes notice of me, since I do so

little here. Perhaps you could care to join me and Nina for dinner sometime next week?"

"Yes, let's do," Margaret said. "She's a lovely girl and well worth your efforts."

Bedros Kasparian, Margaret's employer when she was not chasing after elusive debutantes, had been around the world during the few short months of summer and had indeed acquired any number of treasures to add to the stock of his Madison Avenue antique shop.

He greeted Margaret affectionately. "I'm afraid there is a good deal of work to be done," he said. "Shipments are being released from customs today, and I plan to rearrange the shop. I purchased quite a number of things." He strolled through the simple, tasteful room that served as his showroom and office. "One rather large Buddha from Ceylon, with the original gilt. I may keep it for myself, but I'll display it here. Fabrics, magnificent old kimonos. Some good Indian work from Jaipur. Very nice, although I don't know if there's a market. The ladies who buy and their decorators prefer expensive knickknacks, but the good bits of Ming and Tang are becoming harder to find."

"Have you considered concentrating on a different hemisphere or era?"

"Exactly my thought when I started out," Kasparian said. "I stopped in Africa, but I don't enjoy primitive art as I once did. Any kind of painting has gotten too pricey, and the purveyors aren't the nice sort of people they once were. Furniture is so . . . large." He shook his bald head with its fringe of white. "I am too old to change, so I will stay with the Orient for the time being. Now, what have you been doing since I departed these shores?"

"A couple of murders," Margaret said, "which nobody seems too concerned about."

"Tsk," Kasparian said. His voice was stern, but he had a twinkle in his eye. "I strongly advised you not to get into trouble I presume this gives you opportunity to spend more time with your detective."

"It happened in another state," Margaret said. She did not feel like confessing that there seemed to be some rupture in her relationship with De Vere.

But she did give Kasparian an outline of events as they measured and planned the rearrangement of the showroom.

"You know, Margaret," he said finally, "in my business over many decades, I have seen and heard a great deal. I have heard the Stafford name over and over again. The late Augustus Stafford went through a period of furious buying of valuable objects, as did his father and grandfather before him. It seems that the newer the money is, and the more doubtful the means of its acquisition, the more the possessor of it wishes to have more possessions. I never had dealings with the Staffords personally, but my business has its own grapevine of gossip."

"Yes, but what does that have to do with two murders?"

"Nothing directly," Kasparian said. "Except that a good deal was purchased over the years, and since Augustus Stafford's death—it must be a dozen years ago—a good deal has come back on the market, much of it quite recently."

"Hard times for the Staffords?"

Kasparian sniffed. "Living off their capital, or the proceeds of the sale of accumulated treasures."

"And the land," Margaret said, half to herself. "Why would they need so much money?"

"These are expensive times," Kasparian said. "Perhaps there are unusual financial demands." He surveyed a wall. "The Momoyama kimono could be hung there. A truly beautiful piece. I understand that blackmail is still a cottage industry in most countries around the world."

"Blackmail?"

"It creates an unusual demand for money," Kasparian said.

"So it does," Margaret said. "So it does. And even a good motive for murder."

* * *

"The Staffords?" Poppy said. She shuffled papers. "No problem at all to locate them."

Margaret relaxed in the big puffy chair Poppy liked to sit people in when she interviewed them, although genuine journalistic interviews were rare. Her kind of news was either bits of gossip put together to be confirmed by known facts, sightings of society celebrities at big events by loyal sources, or public relations handouts.

"Let me see . . . Daniel Stafford is on the West Coast. Someone—I can't say who—told me he'd been squiring around one of those young, divorced San Francisco ladies who are queens of Russian Hill out there but not much to speak of here." She looked at Margaret over her glasses. "Does this mean you and he . . . ?"

"Daniel and I were never anything, Poppy. Go on."

"Eloise has taken Camilla to Europe. Shouldn't that child be in school? Anyhow, Eloise has some Parisian friends who choose to believe she is as grand as she claims to be. Augustus pillaged a lot of very fine antiques from the French after the war. That was World War Two," she added.

"People in England remember it quite well," Margaret said.

"Nancy has gone to South America, of all places."

"With her friend Richie?"

"I do not know a Richie," Poppy said. "One doesn't admit to knowing a person of that sort."

"He likes marble," Margaret said.

"Then he should be pleased with Buenos Aires. I understand there is a considerable amount of it there in the public buildings."

"And Toby?"

"Heavens, no one keeps track of him nowadays."

"He claims to give most of his money away."

"Music, the pose of the shabby millionaire, yes. But he's not a generous person as far as I know."

"Perhaps he gives quietly."

"There are no such secrets," Poppy said. "Every conceivable charity has a public relations person to let the world know, so the world can give, too, and feel good about itself. Unless he merely hands out money on the street, but then the press would get wind of it and turn him into a feature story in the Sunday supplements."

"Tell me," Margaret said casually, "what are they saying about Lynne?"

"They? The Luncheon Ladies? Lynne tried so awfully hard to be a society star, but since she never managed to marry Daniel, she was never very important to anyone."

"How did she manage to live so well? I found out that Philip Jordan had several ex-wives who extracted huge divorce settlements. Lynne couldn't have been getting a fortune."

"I don't doubt that Lynne had sources of income we're not aware of. Perhaps there's a family out west. . . ."

"I think not. I think she was blackmailing someone."

Poppy looked wise but close-mouthed.

"So she was! Who?"

"I have no idea," Poppy said. "It's something one has always suspected. She liked to find out things about people, and then use her knowledge. Obviously it worked for the social part, but there may also have been financial considerations. She lived far too well. Could you refer to the Staffords? Are you looking into it?"

"My association with the Staffords has ended," Margaret said. "In any case, it's too late by far for a debut for Camilla, with October on the horizon."

"Certainly the best invitations to all the best parties are ready to be sent, if they haven't been already. The lists of who's coming out at which ball are engraved in stone by this time. She's young, though. Next year perhaps. Although Eloise likes to have things her way, there are some obstacles that not even she can move."

Poppy was wrong, as she seldom was.

"I understand that there are obstacles," Eloise Stafford said. She looked disapprovingly about Kasparian's shop, which was in a state of disarray due to half-unpacked cartons, the looming seven-foot Buddha, and the chattering group of young men deciding how to hang the antique Japanese kimonos to best effect. Eloise looked disapprovingly at Margaret as well, with her touseled hair, blue jeans, and tattered man's shirt that had cost her former husband many, many pounds to have stitched up by his London shirtmaker.

"Madame, this is such an honor!" Kasparian, who never was dressed any way but elegantly, rushed to Eloise, kissed her hand, gently touched her elbow, and guided her to a nearly priceless lacquer and gilt chair at the back of the shop where only the most privileged were allowed to sit. "We are not open, as you can see. Lady Margaret is an angel to assist us. Such an eye. Such taste . . ."

"You know Mrs. Stafford, then," Margaret said. "Mrs. Augustus Stafford."

Kasparian winked a tiny thanks for the clue. "There is no one who doesn't recognize one of our city's great ladies. I understand that you are here to speak with dear Margaret, but you will naturally call on me if there is any service I can provide."

Kasparian effaced himself. The sounds of unpacking and the babble of artistic dissension were miraculously stilled.

"The debut is quite impossible now," Margaret said. She was glad that she had put the Staffords' initial five thousand dollars in a short-term CD, which she would spend, with the interest, on a long and leisurely trip abroad in six months' time. Easter in Rome and onward, until the money was gone.

"I insist that Camilla make her formal debut this winter. You can do it. Indeed, you must." Eloise was looking not so well preserved these days. "I have a private agreement with Camilla. I understand that she confided in you. She will have her money, if she does this for me." Eloise stood up. "My children did not turn out well. I want better for Camilla, who must achieve her small place in society before anything worse occurs. Please."

Margaret had never seen Eloise let her guard down.

Margaret knew she was being foolish, understanding what she did about the Staffords and why two women, even though they were nobody to speak of, should be dead because of them. She nodded her head and agreed to help once more.

"You are a foolish woman," Kasparian said when Eloise had left and Margaret had explained what she had agreed to. "But you are quite a nice one."

Chapter 16

"*My dear* Lady Margaret, it is simply impossible to add another young woman." Mrs. Atherton Whittworth sat comfortably in Margaret's apartment, in her bulky grandeur. She had been in charge of the selection committee for the Junior Cotillion since scaly creatures had struggled ashore from the primordial ooze and discovered the benefits of living on dry land in really well-made frocks with bits of good lace.

"Far too late," Miriam Manson added. Margaret judged that she had evolved a few eons later than the ooze creature but was definitely related.

"She's quite small," Margaret said. "Takes up very little space."

"How witty," said Mrs. Atherton Whittworth, who was not amused.

"And the family is such a good one," Margaret said and poured tea. The photographs of distinguished dukes, minor Royals, Margaret dressed for the hunt, and Priam's Priory in its Tudor splendor were placed so as to be unavoidably visible to the two ladies.

Mrs. Atherton Whittworth pursed her lips. "I have known Eloise for a good many years. My brother was at Yale with Augustus."

"Such a refined man," Miriam Manson said. "We never understood . . . That is to say, when the son married . . . That unpleasantness a few years back, and what did I read . . . ?"

"That will be quite enough, Miriam," Mrs. Atherton

Whittworth said. Margaret noticed that she was especially partial to the miniature mille-feuilles and the chocolate profiteroles that had been laid out for tea. Mrs. Atherton Whittworth had not bowed to the cult of slimness, though all about her contemporaries had succumbed.

"I'd be awfully grateful if you would reconsider... Whatever I could do . . ." She straightened a photograph of herself in a ball gown shot some years before by Norman Parkinson himself.

The two ladies gazed at Margaret. She could tell that they were seeing themselves in the Royal Enclosure at Ascot, curstying to the Queen at a Buckingham Palace garden party, romping among the Highland grouse, chatting up a duchess or at least a countess. Margaret had no reluctance to imply that Priam's Priory was theirs for the asking should their busy schedules permit them to journey to England. Anglophiles are reduced to silliness by the mere appearance of a Cockney chimneysweep, let alone a genuinely titled person, and women like Whittworth and Manson had love of things British instilled in them from the cradle.

To little avail. Margaret had to admit that they turned down Camilla Stafford's plea—Margaret's—with anguish: no palace teas, no Ascot, no waking up in the very uncomfortable bed where the first Elizabeth might have rested her red head briefly on one of her royal progresses. They were sad but firm. The Junior Cotillion was full.

Margaret tried one last ploy. "If you would meet Camilla. She's a lovely girl."

The ladies exchanged a glance as if to say, "So you say, but we know different."

"She's staying here with me for a time. Her grandmother thought it would be good for her." Margaret meant to suggest that she, of all people, could polish up Camilla to a fine luster. In reality Camilla had begged, Eloise had refused, then relented, and Camilla had arrived on Margaret's doorstep only that morning to meet these important ladies. She now hovered in a bedroom, dressed to perfection, hair in place, ready to be accepted as part of the great social whirl.

"I don't think—" Mrs. Atherton Whittworth began.

"Camilla?" Margaret trilled. She was not to be denied by the Whittworth-Mansons. "Come and meet some lovely new friends of mine." They liked that. "If you'll forgive me for saying so," Margaret said mendaciously, as she heard the door to Camilla's room open, "you both remind me so much of my late mother, the Countess of Brayfield."

If that didn't snare them, nothing would.

Camilla had done her part well. She wore a heather tweed suit with sensible shoes, a little string of pearls (her own; Eloise's double strand was promised for the ball), and just a touch of makeup. Margaret had seen to it that her hair had been done by Margaret's own very good hairstylist, and her nails had been manicured beautifully by Josephine herself.

"How do you do?" Camilla said. "I have been looking forward to meeting you. Grandmummy has spoken of you both so often."

Camilla could do it right when she wanted to.

"How nice to meet you," the Whittworth-Mansons said and looked her over very carefully. Margaret repressed an intrusion of jubilation. It was too soon, but Camilla did look like the product of lots of Money (Old), good genes (Stafford side at least), and good taste (attributable perhaps to Margaret's hand). They chatted a bit. Camilla was excruciatingly polite, and only once did her glance flicker to Margaret's direction to indicate how silly all this was.

The ladies seem to soften. Margaret allowed herself to think that success was at hand.

The buzzer from the protective doorman downstairs startled them all.

"Mr. Stafford to see you," said the tinny voice through the speaker.

Daniel might be an asset. He could charm a tree if necessary.

"Have him come up," Margaret said. "Camilla's father," she said to the ladies. "I'm sure you know Daniel Stafford."

"We have met," Mrs. Atherton Whittworth admitted. "Although we don't often mix in the same . . . circles."

Just before her doorbell rang, Margaret had a frightening thought: she did not know that it was Daniel. The Mr. Stafford arriving at her door might be Toby, enough to frighten off any timid dowager who wields a good deal of social power. But Toby had been absent and silent, no doubt defeated by his mother's determination to have a debut for Camilla at all costs. She walked down the hall at the sound of the bell and prayed very hard for Daniel. The ladies were left to admire the ancestral portraits, while Camilla sat with knees and ankles together and looked harmless.

"Hey, Lady Margaret. Long time no see!" Richie's voice boomed out, down the hall and into the alert ears of the Whittworth-Mansons.

"I have guests," Margaret said desperately. Richie was carrying a large box under his arm and was not to be stayed. He pushed Margaret along the short hallway to the living room where the ladies sat. "Nancy heard Camilla had moved in with you, and she wanted to send this box around to her. She wasn't feeling so hot today, so she asked me. You know what women are like when they want something done right away."

He caught sight of Camilla.

"Hey, Camilla! How ya doin', kid?"

"I misunderstood," Margaret explained. "This is not Camilla's father. This is Mr. Richie. . . ." She had never known his surname, and probably just as well.

Richie actually winked at the Whittworth-Mansons. "Like Mr. Marilyn Monroe, right? Nancy's got the better-known name."

"Ah, Nancy Stafford," Mrs. Atherton Whittworth said in a strangled voice. It seemed that she had forgotten that particular blot on the Staffords' history.

Richie thrust the box at Camilla, who took it gingerly.

"Nancy wanted you to have this. I think it's some kind of fancy dress that belonged to your mother."

The expression on the face of Mrs. Atherton Whittworth was one of horror. Miriam Manson had not quite caught on.

"Nancy was helping to clear out Lynne's apartment after she got killed, and this had Camilla's name on it. See?" Written on the box were the words: "For Camilla. Ann's things." "I guess Lynne kept a lot of her sister's stuff after she was murdered. Then she had to get herself killed, too." He turned to Margaret. "You high-class people are worse than some of the guys I know for getting bumped off."

"How nice of Nancy to think of Camilla at this particular time," Margaret said. "And she couldn't have sent a better emissary. You know, messenger."

Since ladies no longer faint or fall into vapors, the Whittworth-Mansons remained upright, if glassy-eyed.

"Don't say your Uncle Richie never did you a favor, kid," he said to Camilla. "And be sure to save me a dance at your debutante thing."

Shortly after Richie's departure, Mrs. Atherton Whittworth made her way, somewhat shaken, to Margaret's door with Miriam Manson following closely.

"Delightful to have met you," Mrs. Atherton Whittworth said. "I don't doubt that we will encounter each other again one day."

Then Margaret's apartment door slammed shut on Camilla's chance at coming out at the Junior Cotillion.

"That's that," Margaret said. "I'm so sorry, Camilla."

But Camilla was looking at the opened box that Richie had brought. Her eyes were wide and scared.

"What is it?" Margaret looked into the box, expecting to see a frothy gown or the like. It was nothing of the sort.

It was a small rug—white with a border of entwined pink and blue flowers, and disfigured by brown stains.

Camilla stared at it, then carefully replaced the cover. "It's nothing," she said. "Some old thing Aunt Lynne wanted to give me."

"Why do you suppose Lynne wanted you to have a rug

that looks as though it might have suited that bare floor in the playhouse? And those looked like bloodstains to me." Margaret had no idea how Camilla would react.

"But she never went there," Camilla said almost desperately. "I mean, she couldn't have moved——"

"You mean Lynn couldn't have moved a body from the playhouse to the solarium where you found it."

Camilla looked down at the floor.

"I don't think she did," Margaret said. "She didn't have anything directly to do with your mother's death. But she acquired the rug somehow, and she used it as some kind of proof that your mother was killed in the playhouse, by someone she knew, and her body was put in the solarium, with a few items taken, so they could make up the story of the intruder."

"Was Aunt Lynne killed because she knew what had happened, and she kept these things?"

"Lynne was killed for more than that," Margaret said. "I don't think she was ever going to tell, because she was blackmailing someone. We've got to have a serious talk, Camilla. There's more than just this rug."

Margaret fetched the silver pendant.

"I want you to tell me about this." Margaret held out the pendant.

"Ohh." It was a slow, mournful sigh. Camilla reached out and took it. "It was Mummy's," she said. "She always wore it."

"I hate to bring back more bad memories," Margaret said, "but do you remember seeing it when you—found her in the solarium?"

"She wasn't wearing it," Camilla said slowly. "Where did you find it?"

"I found it in the garden the night Lynne died. She had it with her when she was . . . killed." Margaret still had a difficult time saying "murder" to Camilla.

Camilla looked down at the floor. "Why did Aunt Lynne have the pendant?"

"I think she found it somewhere, along with the rug, and figured out who killed your mother."

It was a complete story, but there was still something wrong: why did Lynne have the pendant with her that night, after four years? Or did she plan to use it to increase her demands for money? What was it Toby had said? "You've gotten more than you deserve."

Camilla said, "That broken chain I keep in my box is the one she always wore the pendant on. Daddy gave it to her when they were first married. She used to tell me that she said to him, 'I don't want diamonds, I want something simple to remind me that we were simply in love.'" Camilla blinked back tears. "Whoever did it was so angry, they pulled it off her neck."

"Please don't think about it. I'm sorry I had to bring it up, but I needed to know."

"I want to know things, too," Camilla said. "And when I'm through with the debut, I'll be able to find out." The tears were gone. "Can I keep it? I'll take care of it."

What could Margaret do but agree. "But keep it safely in your box," she said. "Someday you will need it."

There was no one Margaret could ask for advice. She would not call De Vere until he called her. Paul would require her to report the matter to someone, if he did not tell De Vere himself. Poor Camilla would end up without her money and her independence, embroiled in the terrible events that must ensue if a member of her family were accused of two murders.

Yet Margaret could not bring herself to ignore the fact of murder forever.

Then she remembered. She had a worse matter to face. She had to tell Eloise Stafford that Camilla would not be allowed to make her debut at the Junior Cotillion.

Chapter 17

"*Then we* shall take another route," Eloise Stafford said. She was surprisingly calm. "I've never cared for the Whittworth woman, and I have an even lesser opinion of Miriam Manson. I shall give a private ball, the way we did in the old days."

"I don't believe even a private ball is possible at this late date," Margaret said. "Everything will be booked from now until the New Year. All the good orchestras, the flower people. I'm sure Josef LeBaron is already working double time, so I couldn't get him. And guests. It was difficult enough to round them up for the party in Cranford. You'll never find young people who are free a single night between mid-December and the first of January."

"But you will, I am certain," Eloise said. She lately had a fanatical gleam in her eye, as though this debut represented the end of the world for her, as perhaps it did.

"It would be very, very expensive," Margaret said. They were meeting at the Stafford townhouse, a place where "very, very expensive" didn't have all that much significance.

"I will see to it," Eloise said. "Have you been seeing Daniel lately?"

"No," Margaret said. "I have been busy." She did not say that Daniel had called her several times, and she had made elaborate excuses. He still seemed intent on developing a long-term relationship, leading to some permanent understanding.

Eloise handed Margaret another check, this one for ten

thousand dollars. "The bank account has been replenished," Eloise said.

With Camilla's money, Margaret thought.

"Now, how shall we manage this ball?" Eloise was businesslike. Margaret imagined that even if she had the slightest suspicion that a member of her family or a minion was involved in two murders, she would never give a sign of it.

"We would have to have a very large room," Margaret said. "A ballroom."

"A pity there's no such room in this house," Eloise said. "So few of my friends have city homes with ballrooms nowadays, and the Cranford house wouldn't be suitable in the winter."

"Then it would have to be a hotel," Margaret said, "but they are undoubtedly booked."

"I shall expect you to resolve the problem," Eloise said. She was reduced to treating Margaret as a servant, which Margaret supposed was only just, since she had pocketed a large fee to do a job of work.

"I'll want Camilla to remain with me," Margaret said. It was the least she could do, protect Camilla a little now that the two of them possessed knowledge of the murders.

"I don't know what to do." In the end, Margaret turned to Paul, who been resourceful in the past about managing to live the good life in Europe before his stepfather had put a stop to it.

"You should ask my mother," he said. "She arrived at the Carlyle yesterday, and she has been most generous to me for a change. Besides, she owns a hotel in New York."

"You jest," Margaret said.

"Not an entire hotel," Paul said. "She invested in one with some partners when she actually examined her hotel bill one day and discovered how high hotel rates now are in the city. It was one of the older places that was stripped down and remade into one of those places with large arrangements of flowers in the lobby and many marble columns. She has modestly named it Villa d'Este, in memory of her Italian interlude with my father."

"She doesn't stay there when she is in the city?"

"Not yet well enough known," Paul said. "And I believe the rates are somewhat higher than at the Carlyle."

"Does it . . . ?" Margaret was almost afraid to ask. "Does it have a ballroom?"

"I do not know," he said. "I avoid any mention of the Villa d'Este in the terrible event that my stepfather decides I am unsuited to banking and tries to introduce me to the hotel business. I believe that would require me to begin by carrying other people's luggage. That is far worse than reading computer printouts about financial transactions in the Persian Gulf."

Carolyn Sue welcomed a companion on a Fifth Avenue prowl, "Jes' to see what they're trying to sell the unsuspecting public," as she put it. "Then we'll run over to Petrossian for a taste of beluga. It makes a nice lunch."

Margaret met her at Bijan, where she was allowed in to watch Carolyn Sue spend several hundred dollars on a new shirt for Ben Hoopes.

"Ben likes the best," Carolyn Sue said. As usual, Carolyn Sue looked as though she knew exactly what "the best" meant. Margaret imagined that Calvin Klein had personally run up her chic little shopping outfit. Her jewelry was so subtle and magnificent that no self-respecting New York mugger would believe it was genuine. "Now, Margaret, what do I hear about you tracking down murderers again? I thought Sam De Vere had forbidden that."

"He has," Margaret said. "To the point where we don't seem to be speaking. Officially there's no murder and hence no murderer."

"I hate to see you and Sam on the outs. Come along, let's look in at Tiffany's and see if there's some little Paloma Picasso brooch I could stand to have. Then we'll hit Bergdorf's, for a quick look."

"I need your help quite seriously," Margaret managed to

get in as Carolyn Sue swung through Tiffany's revolving door. "Do you have a ballroom?"

Carolyn Sue stopped and looked around at her. "Why, yes." The tone suggested that the question was foolish. Everyone had a ballroom. "The Dallas house has quite a big one. 'Course, we use it sometimes for dinner when Ben and I have a few extra people in."

"I mean in New York. Paul says you own a hotel."

"Oh, the d'Este. I don't really own the place, not the way Donald and Ivana own hotels. More like a piece of it. It's managed by this hotel company right in Dallas, so I can check up anytime. They brought in a perfectly lovely man from Switzerland to be the managing director. I knew him years ago. Eric has done wonders with the place. It does have a ballroom. Modest, but nicely done up. I saw to all that."

"I need it for one night between Christmas and New Year's. Every other room is completely booked. I thought you might have"—Margaret smiled as she said the word—"clout."

"It'll be god-awful expensive," Carolyn Sue said. "What do you need it for?"

Margaret explained.

"If price is no object, I could speak to Eric. Maybe he can cancel somebody, especially if you're willing to pay more."

Margaret admired Carolyn Sue's pursuit of dollars.

Carolyn Sue scanned the display cases. "Nothing here I like, and I'm just not in the mood to sit down and have somebody show me things."

By the time they reached Bergdorf's opulent first floor, Margaret was ready to ask her next favor.

"Once we have a ballroom," she said, "we're going to have to fill it. Everyone is so terribly busy around Christmas."

"Offer them something special. The best of everything. Make it sound exclusive. They'll all find a way," Carolyn Sue said. "If Poppy Dill were encouraged to make it sound like nobody is really good enough to be invited . . . Never underestimate the power of good press. I've got friends I can persuade. You have friends. And how about that nice Dianne Stark? She's on all sorts of committees. My, but I wish Paul had taken up with her sister. Could you manage to get a member of the Royal Family across? I suppose not. They all go off to the country to play with their dogs and horses during the holidays. Aldo will go anywhere if his fare is paid. It's been ages since I've seen him." She didn't seem averse to having her ex-husband the prince help Margaret out. "My little Paul is a real prince in his own right, if a mother may say so."

"It might work," Margaret said. "I'll need to pull the pieces together quickly. Time is very short."

"You can count on me to help," Carolyn Sue said. "I always thought it would be real fun to have a daughter coming out. They do some pretty fancy balls down in Dallas. But it is a pleasure that has been denied me." Carolyn Sue was seldom denied any pleasure.

She was also to be denied the pleasure of seeing Prince Aldo.

"My father regrets," Paul told Margaret somewhat later. "He claims business, but he does not have business, so I suspect he is in the midst of acquiring a new mistress and does not dare leave her alone for any length of time. He invites you to visit him when you are in the vicinity of Rome. Although," he added, "I do not recommend the villa during the winter months. Distressingly cold and damp."

Carolyn Sue's influence was evident in the attention Margaret received from the managing director of the Villa d'Este.

"For Mrs. Hoopes, I can arrange anything. Everything," Eric said. "I need not even erase anyone from our schedule. It happens that a wedding that was booked for the ballroom some days after Christmas has unfortunately been canceled."

"How sad," Margaret said happily.

"The groom's first wife discovered that the divorce was not legal and objected strenuously. I think it may mean a larger settlement for her ultimately. These people are so scatterbrained, they fail to take note of whether the papers are in order on those little tropical islands." Eric's Swiss sense of orderliness was offended. Then he shrugged and wrote down carefully the particulars of the Stafford ball.

"Will you want us to handle the food and beverage?" Eric asked. "I don't think any decent catering firm will be available at this late date."

"If you could."

"Delighted," Eric said and wrote some more. Indeed he wrote for a long time, including every possible item that might be required to make Camilla Stafford's coming-out ball memorable in the annals of debdom for years to come.

In the end, Margaret discovered that it was going to be incredibly expensive indeed.

Chapter 18

"*Yes,*" *Paul* said with some resignation. "I will be one of Camilla's official escorts, although I am far too old. It will save me the trouble of explaining to Jytte and Nina why I am not escorting them. Fortunately Leila has taken up with a Moroccan who seems to be related to the king."

"Camilla has asked someone to be her other escort, but she refuses to tell me who it is," Margaret said. "I don't know what other boys she knows. He's probably all right." Margaret shrugged. "She does go out some now that she's staying with me and not subject to constant Stafford surveillance. Donna comes into the city and stays over occasionally. They don't drink or do drugs, as far as I know, and they come home at reasonable hours."

"Have you found it constraining to have her living with you this long time?" Paul was too polite to mention that he was aware that she had not been seeing De Vere even occasionally.

"It has been confining," Margaret said, "but it has been worth it. Camilla has matured in the past couple of months. I have Eloise's confirmation that the papers are signed to allow Camilla to receive her money as of the first of the year. It's not millions, by the way, but it is a substantial sum. She has been talking about going to school to learn useful things to help people."

"For all your suspicions," Paul said, "nothing has come of the idea of murder."

"I have had to let it rest," Margaret said evasively. "Until later perhaps, when the ball is over."

"But you are still convinced, and you have kept silent?" Paul was mildly shocked. "Margaret, you are *pazza*, crazy."

"The Staffords have managed to ignore the fact of two murders, probably committed by a member of the family. Who am I to say differently?"

"You are a law-abiding person."

"I did my best to talk about it to De Vere. He didn't want to listen."

"He didn't want you involved in stirring up trouble where there was none."

"In any case, matters are coming to an end. Soon I'll be gone." The less she saw of De Vere, the more she wanted to go other places: south for the winter, England in the spring. Find a new place to rest and live her life.

"If you still think there is cause to believe in murder," Paul said, "you might still be putting Camilla and yourself in danger."

"I don't have much contact with the Staffords," Margaret said. "Eloise telephones constantly to be kept abreast of the plans. Since she sent Camilla the rug, Nancy has been silent. I wonder if she knew what was in the box."

"What rug is this?"

Paul was nearly speechless when she told him.

"You are mad. This is evidence. Who was it who killed this woman years ago? Nancy? Daniel? Toby? The ruffian who works for Mrs. Stafford? The man who is the father of Camilla's friend? You must not see any of them at all."

Since Paul was so clearly shocked by the news of the rug, she decided it was wise not to mention the pendant at all.

"Toby doesn't show himself, although I know Camilla goes off to his club. Daniel and I now and again have polite meals. I don't know whether he has given up on his plan to make me the wife and mother he so desires. He seems to be waiting."

"For what? To see if you discover who killed his wife and her sister?"

"I don't know," Margaret said.

"It is a conspiracy," Paul said. "We Italians understand conspiracies. The secret meetings, the assassin in the night. You must be very, very careful. I wish you would call De Vere."

"To protect me? He doesn't believe there was any murder."

Now Paul looked at her as though she truly was crazy. "Because there is a strong attraction between the two of you that is being wasted. Besides, you like each other."

Margaret laughed. "Maybe you're right. I'll think about it."

"Don't think too long," Paul said. He was quite serious.

Margaret felt a little jump of panic about what he was trying to tell her. True, she had been busy. True, she was being stubborn in waiting to hear from him first. And true, she had been trying to train herself not to care that something had happened between them to cause a rift. But if he had taken up with someone else . . .

"Is he seeing someone?" she asked.

"He might be." Having given his warning, Paul was being evasive.

"Then I will consider it seriously," Margaret said.

After Paul left, Margaret made a list:

> Silver pendant
> Broken silver chain in Camilla's treasure box
> Blood-stained rug
> Blackmail
> Lovers

Margaret knew quite well what must have happened, but she still did not know who.

Camilla arrived while Margaret pondered her list. She was leading a busy life, with many more invitations to teas and luncheons and parties than Margaret had expected. Eloise was pleased. Camilla also went off some days to do volunteer work for some type of underprivileged or otherwise unfortunate persons, who would probably be the ones to benefit most from Camilla's coming wealth. Since Camilla chose not to inform Margaret, Margaret chose not to pry. By now, however, Margaret was convinced that Toby Stafford had very little to do with charities and a good deal to do with expanding and remodeling his jazz club.

"Your dress was delivered today," Margaret said. Since they were already draining the trusts at a great rate for the sake of this ball, Margaret had not hesitated to buy the best. "Do you want to try it on again?"

Camilla shook her head. "Margaret, sometimes it doesn't seem worth it. I get, like, depressed. I think about my mother. She didn't like all this kind of party stuff, but she would have liked to see me make that big entrance. We'll never know who . . . who murdered her. We'll only know it was someone we know and I don't know if I can live with that."

"Would you be relieved to know who it was, even if nothing were ever done about it?"

"I think so," Camilla said. "Not knowing is hard. I look at them and wonder."

"I have an idea," Margaret said slowly. "I don't know if it will work, but let me explain."

After she had explained, and Camilla had nodded her agreement, Camilla stopped on her way to her room. "I have another surprise for everyone at the ball," she said.

"Harmless, I hope."

"Oh yes." Camilla was suddenly surprisingly cheerful. "Want to take a walk someplace? It's cold but it's nice."

"The decorations at Rockefeller Center. The Christmas windows at Saks. Hot chocolate someplace."

"De Vere, it's Margaret." The cold winter air had cleared her head and settled her mind. Paul was right. Don't delay.

"Yes, well, hello." He sounded a little too hearty. Margaret wished he were in the room with her, instead of far downtown at the other end of a telephone call.

"I behaved stupidly," she said. "And I got stubborn because nobody wanted to believe me."

"It's okay," he said.

"I've missed you. I'm still involved with this Stafford debut, but I need you. Would you please come to the ball? I know you hate the idea, but I do want you there."

"And I want you here, so we can start figuring out why you are such a damn stubborn upper-class wench."

"Why you are a cold-blooded copper."

"Why with my principles, I can be attracted to the upper crust."

"You just like blondes," Margaret said. "I'll find a taxi."

Chapter 19

"*I assured* you that all would be well and Camilla would have her ball," Paul said. He looked magnificent in white tie.

"It's not snowing, if that is what you mean," Margaret said, "although it may be before the night is over." She was a little nervous. She could not imagine the outcome of the plan she and Camilla had devised.

They sat on an extremely comfortable sofa in a sixth-floor suite at the Villa d'Este and waited for Camilla and Donna Kessler to finish dressing in the adjoining bedroom. It was a setting that would have pleased a Renaissance princess, and the cost of the suite would have fed a countryside full of Renaissance peasants for many months.

Someplace below, Matt Kessler waited to dance the first dance with his daughter. Somewhere in the hotel, Richie wore white tie for the first time in his life, and Nancy nursed a private bottle of champagne. Somewhere else, Toby was waiting, and Camilla's surprise escort who was still unknown to all, much to Eloise's disapproval.

"I imagine the family will all be here soon," Margaret said, "to see her before she makes her grand entrance down the staircase."

"Is that done?" Paul asked. "Isn't this rather like a wedding, where the bride makes her spectacular appearance before the assembled revelers?"

"The Staffords don't always do things the usual way."

The door opened. Margaret said, "As I predicted."

Nancy was the first to arrive. She looked quite presentable and alert. Richie had been transformed by formal dress.

"Where's our little debutante angel?" Nancy said. "I'm dying to see how she looks."

"She'll be out in a moment," Margaret said.

"Did you have trouble finding long white gloves?" Nancy asked. "I remember during my debutante season, you couldn't steal a pair, there were so many balls and dances."

"White gloves were obtained," Margaret said.

Eloise marched in, in cream satin, looking almost debutantish herself. "The turnout is exceptional," she said. "Some very nice people managed to rearrange their schedules. I suppose a number of them had planned to attend the Goodman wedding that was cancelled. Even Rom, who is rarely impressed, recognized the limousines outside. Daniel is on his way from the townhouse and will be here momentarily. Prince Paul, I was delighted to see your mother, although she does not seem to have your father with her."

"It would be her husband rather than my father," Paul said, "and Ben Hoopes does not travel well. Like some wines."

Toby and Daniel arrived together. Then came Matt Kessler. It occurred to Margaret that although men complain about wearing formal dress, it enhances their appearance so much that they are secretly pleased with the results.

"I understand my date for the evening is helping the star of the evening to dress," Matt said.

"Hullo, Matt. So glad you could be here, and on good legs for dancing," Margaret said. "Do you know Paul Castrocani?"

"We haven't met," Matt said, "but my daughter is half in love with him." Margaret noticed that all the Staffords carefully avoided conversation with Matt.

"Let's have a drink to get the evening started," Nancy said. She had discovered the chilled bottle of Dom Perignon that Margaret had thoughtfully arranged to have available.

"Was this planned?" Paul asked quietly. "All the suspects in one place?"

"There are no suspects," Margaret said. "There were no murders. Remember?"

Then Margaret's heart skipped the usual beat. De Vere came quietly into the room in perfect white tie. The man who was seldom seen in clothing other than jeans, jacket, and polished loafers looked more of a prince than Paul did.

Toby sidled over. "My brother won't be pleased to see your lawyer friend," he said.

"You are mistaken," Paul said grandly. "Mr. De Vere is a police detective."

"Is he?" Toby said. "No wonder Richie suddenly looks uncomfortable, although to the best of my knowledge, he hasn't been engaged recently in illegal activities."

Margaret had gone to De Vere's side. Toby ran a finger around his collar. "I hate this kind of stupid outfit, don't you?"

"I am accustomed," Paul said. "I believe Margaret and De Vere wish to speak to me."

"How were you persuaded to attend?" Paul asked De Vere. "You didn't mention it to me."

"Your mother is irresistible when she has decided what she wishes one to do," De Vere said. "As is Margaret. In any case, you were off in Dallas for Christmas when I finally bowed to Margaret's pleas during a long walk through a New Jersey snowstorm."

"De Vere's parents were quite pleased that I had civilized him to the point of fancy dress for one night of the year," Margaret said. "And I promised him that I would avoid all types of violent crime in the future."

Margaret hoped he would understand that "the future" meant after this evening.

Eloise said in a loud, clear voice, "What is keeping Camilla?"

The bedroom door opened, but it was Donna who emerged. She wore white with touches of color, as befits the debutante's best friend. "Hi, Dad," she said. "You look terrific."

"So do you, babe," Matt said.

"Where's Camilla?" Eloise demanded.

"Give her a break, Mother," Toby said. "She's not likely to pull a fast one and make a break for it."

"Camilla's real excited," Nancy said. "She won't run away."

Daniel put down his champagne glass and eyed De Vere. He moved closer to the bedroom door.

"I do hope my pearls will survive this evening," Eloise said. "I had to lend them to her, but I do worry."

"They'll be okay," Donna said.

"Mother let me wear the Stafford pearls at my debut," Nancy said. "They made my outfit."

Before Nancy could continue—thank goodness there was something that would silence her—the door opened again, and Camilla emerged, and Margaret held her breath.

All the voices were stilled. Camilla had grown up a lot since the summer, and she had been aided tonight by the combined arts of the very best designer, hairstylist, and cosmetician. She wore a strapless ball gown of pure white satin, classically simple, that showed off her small waist and flared out gracefully behind her. Over it she wore a short white satin bolero to ease Eloise's possible anguish about the strapless bodice. She looked like a genuine princess. There was a universal sigh of appreciation.

Camilla looked Margaret in the eye and smiled faintly. Behind her, Margaret heard someone say, "Oh."

One of them had seen Camilla was not wearing Eloise's pearls, but rather the little silver pendant that had last been worn by Ann Stafford on the day of her murder.

Margaret turned around quickly to see if anyone looked suspicious. She hoped she and Camilla had not made a mistake in deciding the girl should wear the pendant.

"You look beautiful," Daniel said finally. "My little girl."

"Don't get soppy," Nancy said. "You do look terrific."

"We should be going down. Prince Paul . . ." Eloise waved Paul to Camilla's side. "Camilla dear, your other escort? And—" She finally spoke the words. "I trust my pearls are safe."

"Yes, Grandmummy," Camilla said.

Eloise swept out the door, followed by the family.

Margaret waved De Vere on ahead, and hung back with Paul. "It didn't work," she said.

"I do not understand."

"Ann Stafford was wearing that pendant around Camilla's neck when she was killed. Lynne had it when she died. We thought . . ."

"Did you expect a confession?"

"No, but I expected something. . . ."

Camilla looked a little scared as she stopped to look at herself in one of the ornate mirrors near the elevators.

"There may be something yet," Margaret said to Paul. "Keep close watch over her. I'm afraid she—we—have made a statement that someone won't be able to ignore."

"No matter how hard I try to avoid it," Paul said, "you find a way to force me into situations that provide endless trouble."

Eloise was entering the elevator. "Prince Paul, it's time for you and Camilla—and the other one—to take your place at the top of the staircase for your entrance."

"Yes, ma'am," Paul said. Under his breath he said, "And we will enter with as much dignity as we can muster."

"What does that mean?" Margaret didn't like the sound of it. "Do you know who the other escort is?"

"I do," Paul said. "Another prince."

He took Camilla's arm. The party descended. Margaret went back into the suite, into the bedroom. She sighed. Eloise's pearls were lying on the dressing table. She wrapped them in her handkerchief and put them in her evening bag. No point in giving one of Eric's maids an expensive party favor, or at least an expensive temptation. She rode down to the ballroom alone in the elevator and tried to suppress her feeling that things were not going as planned.

Eric and his staff had created a perfect setting. The ballroom had been decorated with simplicity and elegance:

tiny white orchids and white tapers on the tables ringing the floor, which was polished to a gloss that reflected the massive chandeliers glittering overhead. Eric's chef had provided truffles in sauce, and this time the champagne was not modest. Peter Duchin and Lester Lanin had, naturally, been unavailable, but Poppy Dill had kindly exerted pressure amounting to blackmail to persuade a lesser known but acceptable orchestra to play. Margaret had politely turned down Carolyn Sue's offer to round up a few notorious country and western singers who were somehow indebted to Benton Hoopes."

"Back home in Dallas, they'd be a real big draw," Carolyn Sue said, "but I do understand how provincial New York can be." Because Carolyn Sue's annual barbecues were world-famous and nobody wanted to be left out, quite a number of socially prominent New Yorkers had accepted invitations to Camilla's ball simply on the basis of a telephone call from Carolyn Sue.

The ballroom was gratifyingly crowded. Margaret noted that bosoms continued to be in, although some must have been surgically augmented to conform to current standards. Some unfortunate fashion choices were evident in the ladies' gowns, but for the most part it was staid black and white with a touch of red.

The Staffords had assembled at the foot of the broad staircase from the mezzanine to the ballroom. Eric had seen to it that it had been carpeted in blue, and many thousands of dollars worth of the tiny orchids were entwined in the bannisters.

Only a few more minutes, Margaret thought, and Camilla will come into her own. She would soon be gone, clutching her newfound money. Unless Margaret could read guilt and fear on one particular face, the person who had killed Ann and Lynne would be left with only a constant worry that Camilla would return one day to tell her suspicions.

Or that Margaret would tell hers. She'd forgotten that. Since Camilla had been staying with her, it was simple to assume that what Camilla knew, Margaret knew as well.

Margaret hoped they both survived the night.

The orchestra struck up a fanfare of sorts, and most of the guests moved toward the staircase to see the entrance.

"You continue to look beautiful," De Vere said behind her. Margaret looked around at him. There was no man there tonight who looked better than he.

Margaret amended that a few moments later: both of Camilla's escorts, her princes, looked exceptionally fine as they appeared at the top of the stairs—petite blonde Camilla flanked by two tall, dark men.

The only problem was that one of them was probably a bit too dark for the tastes and sensibilities of the evening's guests.

A man standing next to Margaret hurrumphed, the way her grandfather used to hurrumph when the worst had occurred and there was nothing to be done. He said to his companion, "I don't know what the Stafford woman could have been thinking of. He appears to be wearing some sort of order." Indeed, the black man in his formal attire did have a broad colorful stripe of ribbon across his white shirt.

"What do you know?" Margaret said. "This is quite a surprise. How naughty of Camilla. And Toby, I should imagine."

"I should imagine that it is the kind of surprise that causes elderly ladies to swoon," De Vere said.

"I know him," Margaret said. "He is sometimes the bassist in Toby's jazz group, although I didn't recognize him then. But I know him from elsewhere."

The trio descended slowly. There were curtsies and bows and Staffords milling confusedly at the front of the stairs. Although a proper receiving line had been planned, it seemed to have been forgotten. The hiss of shocked whispers almost overpowered the sounds of the orchestra. The guests had certainly been given something extra.

"Well, hullo!" Margaret put out her hand to the black man. "I had no idea you were in New York. Actually I saw you playing with Toby, but I didn't realize who I was seeing."

"Lady Margaret, what a pleasure." The black prince kissed her hand. "I knew you were involved in this, but I was sworn to secrecy. . . ."

Eloise Stafford looked slightly shell-shocked. "Mrs. Stafford," Margaret said, "May I present Prince Mbatu of—"

"You know him? What kind of prince?" Eloise said, effectively demonstrating that she had not lost her ability to remain politely rude even in the most trying of circumstances.

"The prince is from an African country originally, but he was at Oxford with my brother."

"Oxford?" Nancy Stafford elbowed her way in. "Oxford, the university? You never told me that."

"You know this person as well?" Eloise was struggling to maintain composure.

"We've all heard him play with Toby. We call him Mick."

"I had no idea," Daniel said. "I presume Toby—"

"Daniel," Eloise said. "Dance with your daughter."

"I believe that should be the privilege of one of her escorts," Paul said. "And I defer to Prince Mbatu, since he actually has subjects, while I merely trade on my father's name."

"Purely tribal," the prince said, "but you are correct. There are people who feel obliged to obey me, while I understand that no Italian feels compelled to obey any political figure for long."

The prince offered his arm to Camilla, who seemed quite pleased with herself. He led her onto the dance floor, the dance began, and it was a memorable sight for all in attendance.

"How could she? How could she?" Eloise kept repeating.

"He's a hell of a bass player, Mother," Toby said.

"You put her up to this," Eloise said.

"Because some people put Camilla up to sly tricks," Toby said, "it doesn't mean that everyone does." He looked around at Margaret. "I assure you, it was her own decision. They're quite good friends."

"But he's . . . he's . . ."

"Quite a bit older," Paul said. "A mentor of sorts. May I have this dance, Mrs. Stafford?"

Guests began to take the dance floor—Matt with Donna, Nancy and Richie. Toby with a woman in silver lamé, Dianne and Charlie Stark, Carolyn Sue with several men who probably admired equally her healthy blond Texas chic and her reputed millions. Even Leila Perkins put in an appearance with her Moroccan.

"Have we ever danced?" De Vere said.

"I think not," Margaret said, "since you usually refuse to attend dancing events with me, and we did not manage to reach the dance floor in Connecticut at the time of the last murder. Sorry," she added quickly. "The last accident. Although if Lynne were alive, Daniel would have a partner from the family." Daniel could be seen glowering at Margaret and De Vere.

"From what I observed," De Vere said, "Mrs. Jordan was not the partner he wanted." Margaret was pleased to discover that he danced well.

"Nobody wanted Lynne," Margaret said, "and Daniel least of all."

Paul had guided Eloise Stafford to a table filled with her kind: done-up older ladies and their well-nourished husbands. No doubt she was making extravagant explanations regarding Prince Mbatu. She had probably created an entire famine relief program for Africa, with herself and the prince in charge.

"I don't plan to remain long," De Vere said. "I rented this outfit by the hour."

"I understand your pose as a humble man of the people," Margaret said. She looked over the dance floor. "Where has Camilla got to? I asked Paul to keep a watch on her."

Paul was discovered with a buxom young woman who was not well-contained in her dress. "Did you see where Camilla has gone?" Margaret asked.

"She was dancing with various males of her family," Paul said. "I suppose one can consider Richie a member of the family."

Donna was dancing with a good-looking young man. Margaret hated to interrupt. "Do you know where Camilla has gone?"

Donna looked a bit guilty. "She forgot that she left her grandmother's pearls in the room. She went to find them."

"Did she go alone?" Margaret asked.

"I don't know," Donna said. "I saw her with her father and her Uncle Toby over by the doors to the ballroom."

"I have to do something," Margaret said to De Vere. "I'll be right back. Look, there's Carolyn Sue. Doesn't she look sensational? Paul said she bought an extra seat in first class for her gown because she doesn't believe in allowing multi-thousand-dollar Givenchys to fly alone in the baggage compartment."

"Yoo-hoo, Sam!" Carolyn Sue trilled across the ballroom.

"I have never danced with a dress worth many thousands," De Vere said. "I will cherish the experience."

Relieved, as she seldom was, to be free of De Vere, Margaret hurried out of the ballroom to the elevators. Prince Mbatu was at the center of a group of young people listening to his every word. She imagined he was holding forth on jazz techniques for bass players rather than tribal customs of his part of Africa or modern political theory, which had been one of his areas of concentration at Oxford.

Although the Villa d'Este was an exceptionally well-run hotel in most respects, the one flaw might be in its exceptionally slow elevators. She fidgeted as none of the three she faced seemed willing to descend to the ballroom level.

Most probably Camilla was all right, but nevertheless, she wanted to be sure. She had noticed none of the Staffords except Eloise in the ballroom. One of them might be following Camilla to ask about the pendant. Or worse.

Finally an elevator arrived, and took her to the sixth floor and the Staffords' suite. The corridors were not frighteningly long and silent; rather they were short and silent. The door to the Stafford suite was slightly ajar. Margaret pushed it open gently.

Toby Stafford turned around quickly to face her.

She was not surprised to see him. She had expected to find him here and was relieved that she hadn't also discovered Camilla held as his hostage.

"Where's Camilla?" Margaret demanded.

"Gone," Toby said. "Gone back to the ball. She came up here to get Mother's pearls."

"You saw her leave?" Margaret could feel the shape of Eloise's pearls in her evening bag. "With the pearls?"

"Yeah, sure." Toby was markedly uneasy. "She was kind of upset. I think that after the fiasco with Mick ... Mbatu ... Mother told her all deals were off. No money for the child. If she has the pearls, she has something. She can get out if she wishes. Not unlike her own mother in that respect."

"Ann Stafford took what she could from the Staffords and wanted to get out?"

"Something like that," Toby said. Margaret watched him warily. He didn't look dangerous— none of the Staffords looked dangerous—but she suspected they were capable of almost anything.

"It was you Camilla was afraid of. You saw her wearing Ann's pendant, the one that a jealous lover ripped from the chain around her neck when he murdered her."

"I recognized Ann's pendant," Toby said. "I was startled to see Camilla wearing it. She must have seen my shocked expression."

"You knew Lynne Jordan found that pendant someplace —in the playhouse, or hidden away in someone's apartment, or in a jacket pocket. She understood what it meant. She used it for blackmail for four years. Money, lots of money, bought her silence."

"I don't know what you're talking about," Toby said. He made a move in her direction. "You're not afraid of me, are you, dear Lady Margaret?"

"Perhaps I am," Margaret said. "Perhaps Camilla was, too."

"You know that's not true," Toby said. "Are you saying that I killed Ann and Lynne was blackmailing me, so I killed her? And Camilla knew this?" He laughed. "A great story, if it were true. But I didn't kill Ann or Lynne."

"Camilla hasn't taken the pearls," Margaret said. "I have them." She edged toward the bedroom door, but no one was there. The bathroom door stood open; there could be no one hiding under the vast queen-size bed. "And if she's gone back to the ball . . ."

"Margaret," Toby said behind her back. "I didn't kill Ann, but I did love her. Like crazy. Imagine that—in love with your own brother's wife. Lynne found out about us, and yes, she did blackmail me, right up until the time Ann died, because I couldn't let her tell Dan or Mother. They would have cut me off completely."

"But she was also blackmailing the murderer."

"She got greedy before the murder," Toby said. "She had to tell the one person to whom it would matter about Ann and me."

Margaret and Toby looked at each other. "And that person murdered Ann," Margaret said, "and was blackmailed further for his trouble, by the pendant and a bloody rug and the threat of marriage."

The pieces of the Stafford tragedy fell neatly into place.

"It wasn't you," Margaret said, "but you've always known!" She was shocked by her realization that not only had Toby known who the murderer was, but probably the entire family except for Camilla had known as well. "It was the one person who couldn't bear to be humiliated by Ann walking out on him, and who didn't want Lynne as her replacement. It was Daniel."

Chapter 20

Margaret took the stairs and burst into the crowded ballroom, frantically seeking Camilla and Daniel. Or Paul and De Vere. Even Richie.

"Where is everyone? Where's Camilla?"

"Miss Stafford disappeared from the floor some time ago, and seems not to have returned," Prince Mbutu said. "The others?" He shrugged. "Might we have a dance, Margaret?"

"Later, please, Mick. I have . . . an emergency." A matter of life and death sounded too dramatic, however true.

A proper Person in a tailcoat and carnation stood behind the Villa d'Este's front desk and did not seem to understand what the English lady in the frothy ball gown was asking him.

"A young woman in a white satin gown? Running? Here? Yes, I seem to recall . . . She went out the main entrance."

The Person raised his hand and signaled to a bellman. "Escort this lady to the man who sees to the cars," he said.

Margaret said to the man who saw to the cars, "I'm looking for a young girl in a white satin ball gown." Camilla would be running, perhaps believing that her Uncle Toby was a double murderer.

"She alone?"

"Perhaps." It was cold outside the hotel, and a light snow shower had begun to dust the pavement white.

193

"I know the one. There was a chauffeur down the street, sitting in a Lincoln."

"And where are they now?"

"She got in. It's okay, she knew him, the way he opened the door and all."

"Not okay," Margaret murmured. Rom was not a person she would choose to have Camilla safe with. "And she left?"

"Yeah. She got into the car, and it drove up toward Fifth. Then it stopped at the corner and picked up somebody else. Hey, there's the guy now."

The "guy" was Rom, trudging down the cold street from Fifth.

"Where's Camilla?"

"I was taking her back to the house," Rom said, "but Mr. Stafford stopped me on the corner and told me to wait here."

"Mr. Stafford?" Margaret said.

"Mr. Daniel."

"Come," Margaret grabbed Rom's arm and hailed a taxi. "We've got to get to the townhouse."

"Hey, wait . . ." He resisted, she won out.

"Mrs. Stafford would want it. Trust me."

It didn't take the cab long to carry them to the East Side and the Staffords' townhouse. The snow was heavier now, but as they turned onto the street, the Lincoln was visible, parked at the curb in front of the house.

Margaret didn't notice how cold it was as she waited for someone to answer her ring. Finally the manservant opened the door. He wore an overcoat and a hat and carried a small bag.

"No one is at home, madame," he said. "I was leaving."

"Mr. Daniel and Miss Camilla are here," Margaret said. "The car is outside."

"I didn't see them enter," he said. "Ah, Rom. Could you explain to the young lady . . ."

"I got nothing to explain. I was forced to come here." Rom was displeased.

"Then I shall wait for them," Margaret said. The man-servant hesitated. "Lady Margaret Priam."

"I recall you, ma'am," he said. "I just don't know. . ."

"It will be all right," Margaret said. "It's an emergency, actually."

The manservant was uneasy. "Ma'am, Mr. Daniel was here with Miss Camilla. He said . . . he said to say nothing about it to anyone."

Suddenly, from down the block, headlights appeared, and then Daniel's silver Mercedes sped past.

"It's them," Margaret said. "Where did they come from?"

"Mr. Daniel garages his car down the block," Rom said. "I've got to get back to the hotel." He made a move toward the Lincoln.

"Don't you understand what's happening?" Margaret said. But of course he didn't. Then she said, "I suppose you have keys to the Lincoln."

Rom nodded.

"I need them."

"No."

"Miss Camilla is in danger," Margaret said. "I have to follow them. They're probably on their way to the Connecticut house." It seemed the only logical place.

"There's half a blizzard starting," Rom said.

"Look, please don't argue. Daniel Stafford killed his wife, and he killed Mrs. Jordan. You knew he was danger-ous. I think you tried to warn Ann years ago, by leaving her a note in the playhouse. You knew about her going to a lawyer, you probably knew about Toby Stafford—"

"I can't be involved," Rom said. "I got a record. I had to keep quiet." But he gave her the keys. "Ann was good to me. A real down-to-earth person. After she died, I couldn't come out and accuse Mr. Daniel or Mr. Toby."

"But you let Camilla go away with a murderer?"

"He's her father. . . ."

"I know," Margaret said. "I hope that saves her. Go back to the ball and try to locate Prince Paul and Detective De Vere. Tell them where I've gone." She knew that De

Vere would be terribly angry, but it couldn't be helped. She ran through the snow to the car. There was little traffic on the highways leading out of the city and into Connecticut. She drove as fast as she dared, but Daniel in the Mercedes would be traveling much faster.

She played the radio loudly to drown her anxiety. She couldn't imagine what Daniel was thinking. He had killed his wife, and he had killed her sister. What did he intend to do to his daughter?

And to Margaret, someday, somehow?

It had to end somewhere.

It ended at the Stafford estate in Connecticut, where the black, leafless trees lined the drive up the hill, and the fantastic house looked like a huge ghost in the swirling snow.

There were no lights, no evidence that Daniel and Camilla had reached the house. For a moment, Margaret was panicked that she had chosen wrong.

Then she saw a glimmer of light through one of the curtained windows, and as she got out of the big black car, she noticed the Mercedes parked far off by the end of the garage.

She had no plan but to boldly ring the doorbell and wait, shivering under the porte cochere.

The door swung open.

"Margaret!" Daniel seemed stunned at the sight of her. "You shouldn't be here." He looked quite awful. The strain of keeping up appearances at the ball as though nothing had happened, as though the incriminating pendant at Camilla's throat did not exist, seemed to have drained him.

"I had to come," she said. "Camilla is my responsibility. And my friend." He started to close the door.

"You can't come in," he said. "It's too late. I have to explain things to her. Before I go."

Margaret found a reserve of strength and pushed the door. She was in the house. Daniel tried to stop her, but she went by him and across the silent, cold hall to the drawing room. Camilla was huddled in a big armchair, wrapped in a blanket. She looked as though she were in shock.

"Hello, Margaret," she said in a dreamy voice. "Now we know, don't we? Tonight I thought it was Toby, you know, after he saw the pendant, but it was Daddy all the time."

Is he going to kill us? Margaret wondered. She looked around and saw that Daniel was filling a glass from a heavy glass decanter, now quite calm.

"I wouldn't hurt Camilla," he said. He swayed a little. "Or you, unless you make it necessary. I decided to bring her here to delay them. Everyone would be worried about finding Camilla, and they'd forget about me. Give me time to leave."

"Leave?"

"I've been selling off things, storing away money. I knew someday I might have to disappear. I always had plans. I didn't think you'd know it was me."

"I knew from the start that it wasn't a robber who killed Ann," Margaret said. She thought that if she talked slowly and deliberately, and then made him explain, it would give Paul and De Vere time to do something—follow her, call the constable or the State Police. She already knew it was a mistake that she hadn't made those calls herself somewhere along the highway. "And I thought a lot about who could have done it. An angry person who was going to lose an important possession. I thought about Eloise, even Nancy. But it could only have been Toby or you. Toby isn't possessive the way you are. It had to be you."

"She was going to leave me," he said. "And she was having an affair with my brother." He laughed bitterly. "My brother. Lynne was only too happy to tell me all about it." He gulped part of his drink.

"But you were supposedly away from Cranford when it happened." Margaret watched Camilla to see if she was understanding this, but she seemed in a daze.

"I was very near that day, and I had already seen to it that the servants would be off on other business. I came in through the bridle trail, and I prayed I'd catch her with Toby."

"He wasn't there. In fact, their romance was nearly over."

Daniel shook his head. "I met her in that playhouse, and she laughed. I became very, very angry. She talked about divorce, about the lawyer she'd seen. Bob Tannen. I went to prep school with him, and now he knew all about us. I'm afraid I had to kill her, but of course, I couldn't get caught. I couldn't do that to my mother, a son who was a murderer." He didn't seem aware that he was now about to be revealed as a double murderer, rather worse for Eloise.

"So you carried her to the solarium and, after the fact, contrived the story of the intruder. It happened to be your own daughter who found her."

It would have seemed terribly sad, if Margaret weren't worrying whether she and Camilla would end up further victims of Daniel's ego and anger.

"At first I didn't know how Lynne got Ann's pendant. I thought I'd hidden it safely in my rooms at Cranford. But she prowled, she pried, and when she found it, she seemed to understand right away what it meant. She told me she had it."

"She must have found the rug, too."

"That. Ann bled when I killed her in the playhouse. Not a lot, but I had to hide the rug, in case Mother couldn't keep the police in their place. I put it upstairs in the playhouse under the bed until I could burn it, but Lynne pried some more. She actually took it away." He sounded as though the nerve of some people surpassed all bounds of decency. "So I had to pay her the money she wanted, but I wouldn't marry her. That's what she really wanted. When you came along, she threatened. She threatened *me*." He returned to the decanter.

"So you also had to dispose of Lynne."

"She thought I was going to marry you. Mother wanted it, naturally. And I would have married you. But at Camilla's party, she told me to meet her in the garden. I ran into her when the fireworks were going off. She said she'd give me the pendant and the rug as soon as we were married, and if I didn't, she'd tell the world. I hit her with one of the stones along the path. I killed her."

"And tipped over the urn."

"The urn actually was unsteady, you know. I only had to help a little, and it fell onto her body. I was lucky there. It covered up the murder." He was puzzled for a minute. "But how did Camilla get Ann's pendant?"

"Lynne did it to you," Margaret said. "She had it with her in the garden. I found it later, after the body was gone."

"And the rug?"

"It was her last gift to Camilla."

"So you and Camilla did me in. That's that, then," he said. He was terribly disappointed in his women.

"That's *not* that," Margaret said indignantly. "What about your attempt to dispose of both me and Matt last summer?"

Daniel swayed a little. "Merely a warning to you. I like you, Margaret. Matt's a different story. Greedy, like all the rest, and besides"—Daniel smirked—"he once had some idea he could take my wife away from me. From *me*."

"And now you intend to disappear to South America or Mongolia or Alaska, leaving your daughter to face the fact that you murdered her mother and her aunt."

He put down his glass. "I have been making plans. I have a safe island where money eases all difficulties. I was going to leave in the morning, but I think I'll disappear right now. The phone's not connected, so you can't call anyone, and I'll take the keys to the Lincoln, so you won't race down to the village."

Margaret decided that it was the better part of wisdom to surrender them willingly.

Daniel said, "Camilla, kiss your daddy good-bye."

Camilla turned her face away. Margaret could see the tears.

"Dammit," Daniel said. "Look at me. I'm your father." His quiet mood vanished. He grabbed Camilla's arm and pulled her out of the chair. He started to shake her. "If you're going to turn into a bitch like your mother, maybe you'd better come with me so I can teach you proper manners."

"Daniel!" Margaret said in a commanding voice.

He looked around at her, bleary-eyed and unsteady. "Don't you try anything," he said. Camilla stood limp and dazed in his grasp. The tears were flowing freely now. Daniel started to push her ahead of him.

"I hear the sirens," Margaret said. "Detective De Vere has reached the police, and they're almost here. Give it up, Daniel." That there was no sound of sirens didn't seem to penetrate his consciousness.

He didn't answer but started to drag the unresisting Camilla toward the door.

Margaret sighed. True she was wearing a ball gown, and she was tired and cold, and not a little scared, but enough was enough. All through her childhood and adolescence, she'd watched packs of English public schoolboys lay out each other in good fun with classic rugger tackles. She knew how it was done.

Daniel and Margaret hit the floor with a crash. At least, she thought as she went down, the Staffords didn't take up their nice thick rugs for the winter. Camilla, finally coming out of her haze, had the presence to retreat to the windows.

Daniel scrambled to his feet, slightly dazed. He stared at Margaret in stunned surprise. Then he was out the door.

In a few seconds, they heard the roar of the Mercedes. From the window, they could see the sleek silver car backing into the thickly falling snow. Daniel reversed and accelerated and headed down the drive. The tires left deep tracks in the snow.

The taillights disappeared quickly around the bend.

He was too far away from the house when he skidded, veered, and lost control of the car for Margaret and Camilla to hear the crash or see the flames.

Chapter 21

"*Daniel probably* didn't care much about living," Margaret said, "whatever his grandiose plans for running away and starting a new life. And you must understand that I had to follow him for Camilla's sake." De Vere and Paul had found her at the house; the local authorities were busy clearing up the last mess Daniel Stafford had made. Camilla had been whisked away by Mrs. Kessler to spend the night.

" Believe it or not, I do understand," De Vere said.

"And I won't ever do anything like this again," she said.

Paul scowled. He did not believe her, but he was far more accustomed to willful women than was De Vere.

"I don't understand how you knew it to be Daniel," Paul said. "He was—how can I express it?—so cool, so seemingly innocent."

"I think I truly understood when I was contemplating De Vere's silence and my righteous anger over it. People born in a certain class tend to think that all things must go their way. People like Daniel and, I'm ashamed to say, sometimes people like me. There was the divorce lawyer Ann had seen, there were the lovers—although I did not suspect one was Toby—there was Lynne tolerated to a degree that was difficult to understand. Oh, and the art objects sold, the land, the need for money. Toby threw me off for a minute when I found him in the suite. But then I knew."

"Nothing's going to be done about those murders, do you think?" Paul asked.

201

"I think not," De Vere said. "Not that I approve of allowing even dead men to get away with violent crimes."

"I can't even tell Poppy," Margaret said. "She'd be furious if she knew I wasn't telling her the whole story."

"I think," Paul said, "that Miss Dill is smart enough to know that if the father of a debutante dies in an auto accident on the night of his daughter's coming-out ball, and many miles away from the site of the ball, there are questions to be answered."

"Then maybe I'll tell her one day," Margaret said. "She does like to keep her files complete."

De Vere encircled her protectively with his arm as they made their way to his car parked haphazardly under the porte cochere. She leaned her head on his shoulder and yawned. "Please be sure to remind me early to return Eloise Stafford's pearls. I'd hate to be arrested for stealing them by a surprisingly understanding policeman."

12